RF

Books should be returned or renewed by the
last date stamped above

_____

_____

_____

CHARTER MARK

Awarded for excellence

Kent
County
Council

BELLS OF DANGER

Nineteen-year-old Sara Hastings goes to Bruges in Belgium to be nanny to four-year-old Jan Rogier. Oddly, the Rogiers had advertised for 'a very plain girl', so Sara ties her hair in a bun and wears round, old-fashioned glasses. All seems to be going well with the job — until Sara discovers that the previous nanny had mysteriously drowned in the nearby river. Soon, Sara finds her own life in great danger. But who is it who wants rid of her?

DINA McCALL

BELLS OF DANGER

Complete and Unabridged

LINFORD
Leicester

First published in Great Britain in 1985

First Linford Edition
published 2005

British Library CIP Data

McCall, Dina
Bells of danger.—Large print ed.—
Linford romance library
1. Nannies—Fiction 2. Bruges (Belgium)—
Fiction 3. Love stories 4. Large type books
I. Title
823.9'14 [F]

ISBN 1–84395–795–7

Published by
F. A. Thorpe (Publishing)
Anstey, Leicestershire

Set by Words & Graphics Ltd.
Anstey, Leicestershire
Printed and bound in Great Britain by
T. J. International Ltd., Padstow, Cornwall

This book is printed on acid-free paper

1

It was one of those tall, narrow, Belgian houses near the Quai Vert, covered by creeper turning autumnal red. The house itself backed on to one of the many canals that criss-crossed Bruges, but it was impossible to tell from the front, jammed as it was between others.

It's steeply-pointed roof with curved tiles made a warm splash of colour against the blue sky. All in all, it made a pretty picture, and there was no apparent reason why I should get an inexplicable attack of nerves.

It was only a job, for goodness' sake. Being a nanny to a small boy couldn't be all that difficult, and at the age of nineteen, I'd had plenty of experience baby-sitting for the various children of my many cousins. Just because it was a foreign country shouldn't make all that much difference.

Telling myself not to be a fool, I put down my cases and rang the bell. I hardly had time to draw breath when the door opened suddenly.

'Come in, come, come.'

A round dumpling of a woman, dressed all in black, except for a white apron stretched around her ample body and a little white frill of a cap perched on her iron grey hair, almost leaped upon me, taking one of the cases from my hand.

'Oh . . . thank you,' I stammered, not sure how to introduce myself. 'I am Sara Hastings, and I . . . '

'I know.' She waddled ahead of me down a dark hallway. 'I haf been watching out for you.'

Her English was guttural, but clear, and I thanked heaven for that. Two languages, French and Belgian, are used in Belgium, and if I was not mistaken, this woman's native tongue was the latter, of which I did not speak a word.

'I'm very pleased to meet you,' I said

to her retreating back. 'And you are . . .'

She gave a quick glance over her shoulder, and her round face broke into a smile. 'Anna. Call me Anna. I cook.'

So that cleared up that little mystery. I was glad I hadn't greeted her as Madame Rogier. But then, I wasn't even sure whether my employer had a wife. None had been mentioned by the agency, only his name — Hugo Rogier. Perhaps he was a widower. I gave a little smile at the thought. Mother would already be thinking matchmaking thoughts, if she knew!

'Here we are. Come, Sara, sit down. A cup of tea? That is what you English like, ja?'

I sank gratefully on to a chair at the kitchen table. This was obviously Anna's domain. It was as cosy as she was, and I breathed a sigh of relief, suddenly aware how nervous I had become. I don't know why, but that long dark passageway with its hint of unseen rooms behind dark doorways, had been a little daunting. However, nothing could be more normal or welcoming than Anna's kitchen, or her chatter as she brewed a pot of strong tea and set two cups and saucers down on the tablecloth.

Settling herself comfortably opposite me, she said nothing, but her shrewd black buttons of eyes smiled yet took me to pieces. At last, and just as I was growing hot under her scrutiny, she nodded as if satisfied.

'You will be wanting to see the child, Jan. He is playing in the nursery. I will fetch.'

She heaved herself to her feet, and I was left alone. Well, it had all been a bit unexpected, and unsettling, but so far so good. Anna was a nice, motherly soul. It was bound to be a little strange at first, but I would soon get used to it. I sipped my tea, my ears tuned for Anna's return with my small charge.

I didn't have long to wait. She soon came back, shooing before her a small boy of about four years old, clutching the largest white cat I had ever seen. He came to a halt in front of me, and we stared at one another. As I looked at his solemn little face, I was struck by a sudden doubt. Would he understand me? Or did he speak only Flemish?

Then Anna gave him a gentle prod, and he spoke in clear French.

'Bonjour, mademoiselle.'

He had a throaty little voice, that trembled slightly, and it struck me that meeting a new nanny could be a frightening experience for one so young. I crouched beside him, and stroked the cat, who purred loudly.

'What a lovely pet,' I said quietly, speaking to Jan in his own language. 'What's its name? He's awfully large, isn't he?'

He gave me a long look, and then tilted his nose in a gesture of superiority. 'Mimi, and she's a girl.'

'Ah, I'm sorry,' I apologised. 'I suppose you know I'm Sara. What is your name?'

Another long look, and then he

ventured a smile. 'Jan, ma'mselle.'

Obviously somebody had taught him manners. Anna, probably feeling that was enough for our first meeting, took him by the shoulders and turned him around. 'Go find your papa, little one, and tell him Ma'mselle Hastings is here.'

'No need. I can see for myself.'

Scrambling to my feet, I turned to face my new employer. My first impression was that he was a tall man. My second was that he was younger than I had expected, but it was his eyes that held me. They were dark, in a pale, sensitive face that was topped by thick dark hair. He didn't smile at all, just stared me up and down. Then he came farther into the kitchen.

'Let me have a better look at you.' He spoke perfect English. I felt my cheeks beginning to burn as he walked around me.

Wanted, a plain, homely girl as nanny for a small boy living in Bruges, the advert had read. And then,

6

unbelievably, no good-looking girls need apply. A plain girl required.

Well, I'd done the best I could. As soon as I'd arrived at the station I'd found a corner in the ladies' room, and opened one of my suitcases. There were certain alterations I had to make to my appearance. And that, I'd thought with a little shiver of excitement, was what made the whole thing even more of an adventure. It was just as well I hadn't told Mum about it, though.

Out came a flat plain pair of walking shoes, and in went the high-heeled strappy sandals I had been wearing. Out, too, came a three-quarter length jacket of an indeterminate colour I had borrowed from Mum's wardrobe, and in went the bright anorak I was so proud of.

Nobody seemed to pay any attention to my transformation, or if they did, I was too busy to notice. I had to pull back my hair, and tie it into a bun. Long, thick and dark, I thought it my best feature, which was why it had to disappear. I dragged it back so hard, that my eyebrows nearly vanished into my hairline! Then I set to work scrubbing off any trace of make-up. When I had finished, I looked at myself in the mirror with satisfaction. 'Sara,' I'd said to myself. 'You're just what Monsieur Rogier is looking for.'

Now, however, I wasn't so sure, as I stood in that kitchen in my low heels and round spectacles with plain glass that I had bought. At last he stopped in front of me.

'You have remarkably blue eyes,' he said at last.

I was annoyed at being looked up and down like something at a cattle auction.

'I'm sorry,' I replied tartly. 'If I'd known, I'd have changed them.'

Then I stood aghast. What a way to talk to my new employer! What should I say? Apologise? As it was, I just turned redder, and said nothing. At last he sighed and shrugged his shoulders.

'I suppose you'll do,' he said drily.

Then he just turned on his heel and walked out.

I turned in desperation to Anna, but she nodded, as though I'd said nothing out of the ordinary.

'Follow,' she commanded. 'I show you your room. Come, Jan. You come, too.'

We climbed a steep stairway and she opened a door at the end of a corridor. It was a nice room, with high ceilings and a big window at the far end. I went across and looked out. The canal was right below me, the water lapping against the walls of the house.

'I leave you now,' Anna said.

I turned reluctantly from the enchanting scene where the light glinted on the water among the reflections of the tall houses. A boat passed with its load of tourists.

'Oh, Anna, before you go,' I said quickly. 'Tell me, why did the last girl leave?'

Anna stopped in the doorway, her back to me. There was something about her that puzzled me, a frozen air quite foreign to her bustling manner. And the hand that held Jan tightened, until he squealed in protest, pulling his own away, and running off along the corridor.

Anna turned, her face noncommital. 'Other girl?'

'The other nanny,' I prompted. 'The agency said she had left. I wondered why. I mean, if she did something Monsieur Rogier disapproved of, I'd like to know so that I don't repeat it.'

'Oh, no. No!' she said emphatically. 'It was not that. It was ... ' She struggled with the words. Perhaps it was the strain, so much talk in a foreign tongue. 'An upset of the heart. You understand?'

'Oh yes, thank you.' I nodded as though I understood, and she looked relieved.

'Good. I go now. There is dinner to prepare.'

I was glad to be left to myself. There was so much to take in, so much to think about. First, there was the room itself to explore. The bed was high and hard, covered by a white crocheted coverlet. The wardrobe was vast, of dark wood, heavily carved. There was a matching chest of drawers large enough to have taken all the clothes I'd ever owned, let alone the contents of my two suitcases.

I dumped them on the bed, and started putting my things away. I hadn't brought *all* dowdy clothes. I reckoned that once the family got used to me, I'd start introducing my ordinary things, and Monsieur Rogier would hardly notice.

As I hung up my skirts and sensible blouses, I began thinking about my new employer. He wasn't at all what I had expected. Somehow, with all that talk about a plain, homely girl, I had imagined somebody stiff and pompous. And he hadn't been like that at all.

I sat on the bed, a pair of shoes in my hand, and thought about him. He looked quite young, no more than his early thirties, at the most. He'd been dressed casually, brown corduroy trousers and a soft checked shirt, open at the neck. But the thing I remembered most was the intensity of his eyes. I wasn't sure of the colour, except that they had been dark, but I couldn't forget the piercing quality of that gaze. It had made me feel quite weak.

I jumped to my feet, and shoved my shoes into the wardrobe. Enough daydreaming. Perhaps that was what had gone wrong with my predecessor. Had she fallen for her boss, I wondered. If she had, well, I could hardly blame her. But what had she done that was so awful that he had to protect himself from good-looking girls?

Whatever it was, I would be careful not to fall into the same trap. I wasn't here to have any 'upset of the heart' as Anna called it. Quite the contrary, in fact. All I wanted was to see a bit of the world and to have fun.

My suitcases emptied, I stuffed them into the other half of the wardrobe

— there was ample room — and looked around to see what I should do next. There was a wash-basin in the corner, with a mirror attached to the wall so I took the opportunity to freshen up. It was nice to let my hair down for a moment, literally.

I brushed it vigorously, letting it swing around my face. Hugo Rogier had been spot on about my eyes. They were quite startling. Sometimes I wished they had been lighter. They dominate my face, giving me a little-girl-lost look, that I insisted was at variance with my real character.

'Sara, you're not as tough as you think,' my mother liked to say.

I paused in my brushing, and for a moment felt a pang of homesickness as I remembered the way she'd fussed the night before — only hours ago, really.

'But I don't *want* to settle down yet.' I smiled reassuringly at her as she sat glumly on my bed while I finished my packing. 'Belgium isn't the other side of the world, you know.'

Mum watched me quietly as I folded clothes and put them into the open suitcase.

'You'll need some thick sweaters,' she remarked. 'It's September, remember, Sara. Summer is nearly over.' She paused for a moment, and then returned to the attack. 'It seems far enough away to me. And what attracted you to the idea of becoming a nanny?'

I fought back a sigh. I'd been out of work for six months, with no sign of a job on the horizon — or at least, not an interesting one — not until then. I pushed back my hair, which as usual had fallen forward over my eyes, and tried to be reasonable.

'It wasn't my fault that Goodings closed down and left me jobless.' A finger of excitement touched me, and I turned to her eagerly, wanting her to see things my way. 'I'm lucky to have this opportunity. Don't you see? It means I can perfect my French, and perhaps that will lead to something better. Lots of firms want linguists these days.'

That was really just to pacify mother. I wasn't thinking too much about my future career prospects. It was enough to be doing something different. Something exciting. Anything, to get away from home and spread my wings.

My mother sniffed. 'And what about Derek?'

I froze for a moment, and then went on debating whether or not to pack my jeans. Derek was part of the reason I wanted to leave. We'd known one another since childhood, and perhaps I had drifted into imagining that it was a great love affair. I hadn't long discovered that Derek had no intentions, other than a brotherly affection. It had only been the families pushing us, not least my own mother.

'What about Derek?' I asked.

'Well, you know,' Mum said vaguely. 'Your father and I have always thought . . .'

'Ah,' I said vaguely, making a decision and folding in the jeans, snapping shut the lid of my case.

'But he's such a nice boy.'

Another well-used phrase of my mother's and I couldn't help giving an amused grin. 'Yes, he is. He's all that, but he isn't for me.'

Relenting, I placed the case on the floor and put my arms around Mum's worried shoulders. 'Don't worry about Derek. He's got other fish to fry . . . really!' I gave her a quick hug, and changed the subject. 'Don't you and Dad wish me luck?'

Her arms went tightly around me. 'Oh, Sara, love. You know we do. But . . . ' Another huge sigh. 'I wish you weren't going to somewhere I've never even heard of. I do hope you know what you're doing!'

I came back to the present with a bump, and tied my hair back into its severe bun. I knew *exactly* what I was doing. I was stepping out on my own, and at the age of nineteen, it was high time I did.

I'd been lucky to find this job. I didn't really have any qualifications, but I had a friend at the agency who had

16

put in a word for me. And now, there was a whole new world waiting for me out there. Bruges promised to be everything I had imagined it, and more. The glimpses I had seen from the taxi had been intriguing — little cobbled streets, narrow canals and charming hump-backed bridges.

I settled my specs back on to my nose, and took one last look in the mirror. I could only see the top part of me, but knew that my skirt was suitably long, and the dull blouse did nothing for my looks. I grinned at myself in the mirror . . . and then froze.

In the reflection, behind me, I saw the bedroom door opening slowly. It was just a crack, enough for someone standing on the other side to squint through. The back of my neck went all cold and prickly. Then I laughed.

'Jan?' I said happily. 'Come in. You don't need to stand out there. I won't bite. Honestly.'

But the door didn't open any farther. I swallowed nervously. 'Jan, is that you?'

Then with a speed that made me jump, it swung open. A woman stood framed in the doorway. She was tall and slender, sheathed in a slinky black dress with long close-fitting sleeves and a high neckline. It was striking in its simplicity.

In my surprise, I just goggled at her. Her hair was cut short, a thick shining cap of gleaming silver, but the face it framed was only young. A strong face, with high cheekbones, a perfectly-moulded scarlet mouth, and clear, green eyes that inspected me, narrowing a little as she looked me up and down.

My first impression was how beautiful she was and then how cold. I'm not usually ill at ease with people, but she made me all tongue-tied. She was so beautiful, and somehow so unnerving.

But I was proved wrong, because then she smiled at me, and the uneasy feeling vanished.

'I'm sorry,' she said. 'Did I startle you?'

'You did rather,' I admitted. 'I suppose it's because I'm so new here. I'm Sara Hastings, Jan's new nanny. I suppose you must be . . . '

'Maxime Rogier, Jan's mother.' Still smiling, she glided farther into the room, holding out her hands to clasp mine warmly. 'Hugo's right. You look most suitable.' Then she tucked her arm in mine.

'Come along,' she said sweetly. 'Anna has dinner ready. You will dine with us, of course. Jan eats with us, too. I rely on you to keep him in order.'

Her laugh rang out.

'Of course,' I said eagerly. 'I'm sure it's been difficult for you since the last nanny left.'

She dropped my arm. 'Who told you about Helen? What d'you know?' she asked abruptly.

'Why, only that she left because of boyfriend trouble,' I stammered.

She smiled at me again. 'Ah, yes . . . well, we don't want any more of that, do we?' She chuckled. 'I'm sure you won't be any trouble at all.'

She took my arm again in a friendly way.

'We're all going to be one big happy family. I can feel it in my bones. Come along now, my darling husband will be waiting.'

2

The dining-room lay behind one of the doors in the dark hallway. Jan was already there, talking to his father.

'Sit on your chair, Jan,' Madame Rogier said. 'Sara, you may sit next to him. Hugo, dear, will you ring for Anna?'

It was a strange meal. I felt ill at ease with these people who were, as yet, complete strangers to me. Maxime Rogier was charming, but her husband — apart from giving me a very searching look — ignored me.

I didn't need to keep Jan in order. For such a small child, he was very well behaved, and sat up to the table with the adults, balanced on a cushion.

'Have you ever been to Belgium before?' Maxime asked. 'You speak very good French.'

I explained that this was my first

visit, but that I had liked the little I had seen. Hugo Rogier looked up then, and gave a rare smile.

'Then you must explore. You will find Bruges a beautiful city, and full of interest.'

I was just registering the way his face lit up, and how much a smile changed his expression, when his wife interrupted. 'Of course,' she said with a shrug, 'Bruges has its charm, but it is very limited. Not like Paris.'

'My wife is French,' Monsieur Rogier explained.

'Ah, Paris!' she went on dreamily. 'Now, France is the true centre of civilisation. The theatre . . . the opera . . . '

'We do have those here, Maxime.'

For a moment, her eyes seemed to flash. Then she turned to me sweetly. 'Hugo was born here. Naturally he is very partisan.' She turned to her husband. 'You should show Sara some of the sights, darling.'

He gave me a frown. 'I'm really too busy,' he said curtly. 'Jan should be taken out each day to get some fresh air. Let Sara explore while she is with him.'

* * *

'Can we take a boat trip? Can we, Sara?'

Jan's hand tugged at mine, and I looked down at the little figure by my side and smiled.

'Why not, my little friend? I'd like that, too.'

I had been in Bruges for only just over a week, and already I'd come to live for my daily excursions with Jan. Anything to get out of that dark house on the Quai Vert, though I couldn't really have said why.

Everybody had been nice to me. Anna fussed over me as though I was her own daughter, Jan had been no trouble, and Hugo Rogier had, for the most part, been polite. Madame Rogier, or Maxime, as she insisted I call her, had been sweetness itself.

So why was I here, standing at the little bridge by the Djiver, so pathetically grateful for the heart-warming glow of the red-creepered walls of the houses, the gay umbrellas of the tables outside the tea-rooms.

'Come on,' I said. 'There's a boat just ready to leave.'

There were just two seats left, and as Jan and I stepped aboard, the other passengers inched up for us. They were all tourists, judging by the cameras hung around their necks. We pushed off from the mooring place, and as we did so, I glanced back at the bridge that spanned the canal.

I grabbed Jan's arm. 'Look, there's your daddy on the bridge.'

'Where, where?' He scrambled to his feet, and I had to restrain him.

'No, he's gone now. I'm *sure* it was your father.'

Jan shook his head wisely. 'I don't think so, ma'mselle. Papa will be in the office now.'

He was right of course. There was no

reason for Hugo Rogier to be there at this hour of the morning. And yet I could have sworn the man on the bridge had been him. I got the impression that he had been watching us. So why hadn't he waved? Why had he turned and disappeared the moment I pointed him out?

'Yes, I must have been mistaken,' I said slowly and turned my attention to the passing sights as our trip got under way.

'This is fun, isn't it, Sara? I like boat trips.'

I agreed with Jan, it was great fun. It made it all worth while, the dowdy clothes and the way I had to look. I had to admit it was beginning to pall a bit, now that the novelty had worn off. I would have given anything to revert back to my old self.

I couldn't see why I had to disguise myself in this way. It wasn't as though Maxime was the sort of woman who feared competition. And, for most of the time, Hugo Rogier didn't appear to notice me at all, or if he did, he was indifferent to the point of being rude.

Yet, for all that, there were times when he could be friendly. Only the day before, he had chanced to come into the kitchen while I was there chatting to Anna. He had joined in, asking me all sorts of questions about my home, my parents, my interests. As I found myself laughing and joking with him, I realised that he had a charm that would be hard to resist.

Then Maxime joined us, and he had changed completely.

'Shouldn't you be with Jan?' he had asked me curtly. 'We do employ you to look after him, you know. Not to stand about gossiping with Anna.'

I'd stood blushing and stammering in confusion, and it was Maxime who had rescued me. 'Don't be such an old grouch, darling,' she'd scolded. 'Jan is perfectly happy in the nursery. He's doing a drawing for Sara. Now come along, let the girls have their chat.' And she'd led him away.

'Sara!' Jan was tugging at my hand again, to gain my attention. 'Can we go on a boat trip down the big canal one day. The one that goes to Damme? I've never been there. Helen didn't take me.'

My attention was caught immediately. 'We'll see.' Perhaps I would get a little more out of Jan than I had from the rest of the household. 'Did you like Helen?'

He gave a shrug that was a shadow of his mother's. 'She was rough when she washed my neck.' He paused.

'But she laughed a lot.' Then he changed the subject as something caught his eye.

Nobody seemed to want to talk about Helen at any great length. Anna avoided the subject, and I hadn't liked to bring it up again with Maxime. It intrigued me. Had Helen been sacked, or had she left of her own free will? And who had been the cause of the romantic upset?

Surely not Hugo Rogier! He hardly

27

seemed to me to be that kind of man. Certainly, he had never been anything but polite to me, though I had caught him looking at me once or twice . . .

Oh, enough of this! My imagination was running away with me. Helen had probably left a boyfriend in England, and had pined for him so much that she had returned there without much notice. Perhaps the Rogiers thought that if they employed a plain girl, they were less likely to be left in the lurch again. I settled down to enjoy the rest of the trip.

'Now what shall we do?' Jan demanded at the end of the trip. We had returned to the landing-stage and stepped ashore with all the other tourists. As we did so, the sound of bells rang out through the clear morning air. I stood, entranced.

'Come on!' Jan was becoming impatient. 'Sara, why don't you come?'

'Wait a minute. I'm listening to the bells. You listen, too, Jan.'

To Jan it was commonplace, something he had known all his life, but to me it was a source of delight. Every day the bells at the top of the tall Halles Tower played a different tune. They could be heard all over the city. It was part of the charm of Bruges.

I glanced at my watch. Only eleven o'clock.

'Shall we go to the Grand Place? We can hear the bells even better there, and I will buy you a lemonade.'

Jan was happy with the suggestion, so we set off towards the Grand Place. Just then, I spotted Hugo Rogier coming towards us.

'Papa!' Jan saw him, too, and ran to him. Monsieur Rogier caught him and swung him into the air, laughing.

'Papa, Sara's going to buy me a lemonade.'

His father looked at me over Jan's head and his face creased into a smile. 'Then perhaps I can persuade her to buy one for me, as well?'

He was joking, of course . . . wasn't he? I didn't know what to say, but he fell into step beside us. Jan skipped between us, and insisted on holding our hands. I walked in silence, feeling awkward and even more frumpish than ever.

It would have been quite different if I had been my old self. I'd never been tongue-tied before, quite the reverse. It seemed as though putting aside my own clothes had lost my character. The new Sara Hastings felt nervous and unsure of herself. And anyway, this man was so much a man of the world. And, I hastened to remind myself, he was married.

'Shall we sit outside, here at the pavement café?'

We had reached the Grand Place, just as the bells came to a halt. Jan and I were indicated chairs under striped umbrellas, while Monsieur Rogier ordered. I sat, taking an exaggerated interest in the cars parked in the square. He looked puzzled, and then his brow cleared.

'Do you see the flower-sellers over there, underneath the arches of the Halles. They're here all the time.'

By twisting around in my seat, I

could just make out the baskets piled high, bright splashes of colour in the shade of the archways. It gave me something to look at and talk about until the waiter came with the lemonade and two frothing, creamy coffees.

'Thank you, Monsieur.'

'Please,' he interrupted. 'I have heard you calling my wife Maxime. Can you not call me Hugo?'

I gulped my coffee. Was this how he had begun with Helen? I remembered seeing him earlier on the bridge. Perhaps he had been following me, just to get me alone. This was where I had to show my employer, nicely but firmly, that he was wasting his time.

'Thank you, Hugo,' I said meekly instead.

'It is a pleasure.'

His eyes, I discovered, were not really brown, but a very, very dark blue. And he had little laughter lines radiating from them.

'Tell me,' he said as though he was really interested, 'how much of Bruges have you seen so far?'

He was easy to talk to, so easy that I soon forgot my ridiculous fancies. Looking at him, relaxed and at ease, talking with enthusiasm about the Groening Museum and the Beguinage Convent, I couldn't imagine why I could have thought such things about him. He was a happily married man.

All the nicest men are, I thought glumly. Available ones seemed either stodgy and uninteresting, or brash and self-seeking. You never found one like Hugo who was also unattached. As he was talking about all the places I should see, I found my thoughts wandering. I had to draw myself up sharply as I found myself staring at him.

'Aren't you working today, Monsi . . . er . . . Hugo?'

He blinked at me for a moment.

'Of course. I have just come from my office.'

'I told her,' Jan piped up. 'I told her you were in your office. Sara said she saw you on the bridge, but she was wrong.'

For a moment, Hugo's eyes dropped, but then he smiled.

'You were probably both right. I had had enough of work. It is such a beautiful day, perhaps one of the last we shall get this year, and I felt like a breath of fresh air. That is one of the glories of being your own boss.'

'Where do you work, Hugo?' I asked.

It turned out he owned an art gallery in the Zilverpand, a prestigious shopping precinct. I'd heard about it, but I hadn't explored it as yet.

'I must find it.' I laughed. 'I'll take the street map with me. I suppose there are boutiques. I just love shopping for clothes.'

My voice tailed off, and I could feel my face going red. When I stole a glance at him, he had just the trace of a smile.

'Of course there are boutiques. Bruges knows how to cater for pretty girls.'

He had seen through me, I was sure. A hasty glance at my watch, and I was on my feet.

'Come along, Jan. It's time we went home. We don't want to be late for lunch.'

Hugo stood politely as I urged Jan to finish his drink then wiped his mouth.

'Then I will see you tonight, at dinner. I must return to work now.' For a moment his eyes looked into mine, and then he looked away. 'It would not do if Maxime thought I had been shirking.' He gave a little laugh, and turned to go, then swung on his heel. 'Thank you,' he said seriously. 'Thank you for sparing a few moments of your time. I have enjoyed it. It has been like a breath of fresh air.'

He paused only to ruffle Jan's hair, and then he went away, walking briskly across the square without a backward glance.

Had that been a warning I wondered uneasily? A hint that I should not mention our coffee together? As Jan and I walked back to the Quai Vert, I kept thinking how much I disliked this. Somehow it spoiled everything. I, too, had enjoyed the few minutes at the pavement café. There had been nothing wrong about it. We had only talked of museums, of paintings, of things of beauty. If there had been, on my part, a feeling of pleasure at being with him, that was absolutely my own affair. Nothing he had said or done demanded secrecy. So why should I feel so guilty?

That evening, at dinner, I felt bold enough to experiment by wearing one of my own dresses. It was nothing special, just soft wool in a shade that matched my eyes. It was hardly likely that I would be dismissed, just because I'd stopped looking like a sack of potatoes. I even put on my sandals, although I still scraped back my hair and wore my glasses. As I left my room and went down the stairs to the dining-room, I felt pretty confident that neither Hugo nor Maxime would say a word.

As it happened, I was right, but only because Jan got in first! I might have known. Children always land you in it.

He was already perched on his cushion, and as I took my seat, and Anna brought in a salmon salad, he beamed at me.

'Is that a new dress, Sara? Did you buy it at a shop near Daddy's, like he told you this morning?'

The silence was embarrassing.

'No,' I said at last, as casually as I could. 'I brought it with me, Jan. I've had it a long time.'

I could see Maxime looking at me thoughtfully. 'But I *will* visit the Zilverpand one day,' I said lightly. I smiled at her, and could only hope I looked as innocent as I undoubtedly was, even if I didn't feel it. 'We were lucky enough to bump into Monsieur Rogier this morning,' I explained. 'He bought Jan a lemonade.'

This was not the time, I thought, to go into how long we had chatted over coffee, or to call him Hugo. I needn't have worried. She wrinkled her nose at me.

'I'm glad to know he doesn't spend

all of his time working.' She patted Hugo's arm playfully. 'You're becoming quite a workaholic. It isn't good for you, Hugo. You've been quite morose lately.'

She had a point there. He was glowering at his plate as though the food had offended him. He seemed tense and edgy, a different man from the eager, vivid person I had talked to that morning.

What happened next was definitely evidence of his frame of mind. We had just finished our sweet of fruit salad with ice-cream and Jan had been given leave to get down from the table. Mimi, Jan's white cat, stalked in looking for titbits, and Jan descended on her with a glad cry. He gathered the cat into his arms, and it rubbed her face against his and purred.

'Really child,' Maxime said, 'you're besotted by that cat. I think you love it better than anything.' She laughed, turning to me. 'I honestly think it means more to him than I do!'

'It's unhygienic to have it in here,' Hugo thundered.

He was on his feet, his face scowling. He pointed at the poor cat, shouting, 'Get that creature out of here, Jan. And don't let me see you touching it again or I'll get rid of it. Do you understand?'

He was really shouting. Jan stood amazed, his lower lip quivering. The cat escaped from his arms and went running out of the room. Quietly I pushed my chair away from the table.

'If you'll excuse me, I think I'll go up to my room. I have some letters to write. Come along, Jan. Come with me.'

What, I wondered, had brought that on. Hugo hadn't worried about the cat before. Jan was always petting it, and his father hadn't objected. Indeed, I had seen him stroking it himself, many times. Had he simply been venting his bad temper because Jan had spilled the beans about our morning meeting?

It was a depressing thought. Life here was becoming complicated. No wonder my predecessor had left. I collected my writing things and sat down on a chair at the window, looking out on the canal. How could a man change so much? But then, why should it matter to me? He was my employer, nothing more. There was a light tap at my door.

'Come in,' I called, expecting it to be Anna, who often came up for a chat.

But it was Maxime. She entered hesitantly, not quite as poised as usual. 'May I talk to you?' she asked softly.

I invited her in and she sat on the bed. For a moment, she bowed her head, the evening light shining on her hair. At last she looked up.

'I don't know how to say this Sara, without offending you.'

There didn't seem to be anything to say, so I kept quiet. She cleared her throat.

'I . . . er . . . I just want to warn you, about Hugo,' she went on.

I felt my throat going dry. 'About Monsieur Rogier?'

'Yes.' She made a helpless gesture

with her hands. 'Oh, I'm quite sure this morning was innocent. My husband has an eye for the girls. That does not worry me. But please be careful, my dear. You saw tonight how changeable Hugo can be.'

She rose to leave, and then paused. She looked me full in the face, her green eyes wide and worried.

'I wouldn't like there to be another tragedy.'

3

It wasn't surprising I didn't sleep well that night. The house seemed gloomier and more mysterious than ever, and I lay awake until the small hours of the morning, staring into the darkness, my mind going round in circles.

What had Maxime meant about Hugo? I couldn't believe what she said. He was not the sort of man who chased girls just for the fun of it, I was sure of it.

And yet, if it was not true, then Maxime had been lying, and why should she suggest such a thing about her own husband? It didn't make sense. There was something they weren't telling me, something to do with the girl whose place I had taken.

Yet, Hugo's outburst that evening had been very strange. I remembered his expression as he had shouted at poor little Jan. Funnily enough it had not been one of anger, more a kind of desperation and dread, so very different from the pleasant man whose company I had enjoyed that morning.

I jerked awake, and realised I had been dozing, but I knew I had not woken naturally. Something had disturbed me. I had drawn back the curtains at the long window, and the moonlight shone across my bed, spilling over on to the patterned carpet. I sat up and swung my legs out of bed and groped for my slippers. Then I took my robe from the hook on the back of the door. I stood for a moment, listening.

All seemed quiet. I must have been imagining things. I shivered and pulled my dressing-gown tighter around me. Then I heard it again!

It was a woman's voice — Maxime, I was sure of it. It only took me a second to reach the bedroom door and open it. Yes, it was Maxime, screaming. Although I couldn't make out the words, I could hear shouting, even though hers and Hugo's bedroom was on the floor above. There was the deeper voice of Hugo, then Maxime again, sobbing. Then silence. I remembered what she had said to me, just before she left my room, and I shivered.

Everything was now deadly quiet. Then farther along the landing, Anna's door opened. She came over to me when she saw me in the shadows.

'Sara, what you do out of bed?' she whispered.

'Anna, did you hear that? It was Maxime. Whatever is wrong?'

She pushed me into my room, and closed the door behind us. 'Close the curtains, child,' she said, and as I did so, she switched on the light.

I turned to face her and almost laughed with relief. Nothing could have looked more homely or comforting. Her ample figure was enveloped in a floral, quilted dressing-gown, her hair screwed up in curlers and topped by a thick net that came down over her forehead. I could see she was definitely worried.

'Anna, what *is* going on?' I repeated.

She patted the bed. 'Climb in, Sara. You'll catch cold.' As I did so, she sat on the bed beside me. 'You heard Madame Rogier, ja?'

I nodded.

'You must not be upset. It is nothing,' she assured me.

'What d'you mean? It sounded as if she was being . . . '

I stopped when Anna began shaking her head.

'I told you,' she said. 'Madame Rogier gets upset at times. She is, how you say it, high strung, ja?'

'Yes, but . . . '

'Before Jan was born, she was opera singer. Very famous. Men courted her. Then she met Monsieur Rogier, and he won her, and in a little while Jan was born.'

I could see it all now, I should have guessed Maxime was special. There had been something theatrical about her,

44

even the first time we had met, when she made such a dramatic entrance.

'The birth was not easy,' Anna continued. 'And afterwards, she was ill for a long time. There came much depression. The doctors warned she could not stand the rigours of an operatic career.'

She pursed her lips as if there were things she would have liked to say, but thought it better not to. 'Madame had to settle down to being a good wife. But sometimes, she becomes upset. Monsier Hugo is very patient. You understand?'

I understood that Anna was very loyal to Hugo. Perhaps she even resented his beautiful wife. I found myself feeling sorry for Maxime. It must have been hard to lose the career she loved. I remembered the ecstatic look on her face when she had spoken of Paris, and the opera there.

'Come now,' Anna said briskly. 'Lie down and go to sleep. It's your half-day off tomorrow, is it not? You want to be at your best to enjoy it. You must not let tonight upset you. It is nothing.'

There was no arguing with Anna. She tucked me up and switched off the light, and before I could object, she had gone. I found myself yawning. Her explanation had taken away some of the uneasiness I had been feeling. It was none of my business really. I fell asleep so quickly that I forgot I had never asked Anna what Maxime had meant by 'another tragedy'.

I awoke at six o'clock. Breakfast was not until eight, and Jan would not stir for at least another hour, so I could enjoy my lie in.

That morning, however, I found I was too restless to lie there, doing nothing. I rose and pushed up the bottom half of the big sash windows. The air smelled cool. Later, I thought, I would go out alone and explore the city. I would be able to go farther afield, and cover more ground without little Jan. I was looking forward to it.

I washed and dressed, dragging my hair back without a second's thought. It had become so much of a habit now. Then I decided on a cup of coffee. The house was very still as I walked down the stairs.

The kitchen was welcoming and bright, every surface gleaming and spotless. Anna would not mind me invading her kingdom, I felt sure. I took a cup and saucer down from the pine dresser, and filled the heavy old-fashioned percolator with freshly ground coffee. Mimi was stretched out on the floor, and I stepped over her, to reach the socket.

'Out of my way, cat,' I scolded. 'What a silly place to sleep. Why aren't you in your nice comfy basket?'

She was so fast asleep, she didn't even twitch a whisker. I waited until the coffee was gurgling away, then decided that maybe one of Anna's home-made biscuits would go down very well.

But I'd forgotten the cat, and as I turned, I nearly fell over it, catching it with my foot.

'Oh, Mimi, I'm sorry!' I hesitated. 'Mimi?'

She hadn't moved at all. No angry miaow, not even an indignant paw. I had to force myself to kneel down and touch her, but even before I did so, I had a horrid foreboding of what I would find.

'Good morning, Sara.' A cheerful voice boomed out from behind me. 'You're up early. Gracious me, what are you doing down there?'

Still crouching beside Mimi, I swivelled around to face Anna. I fought back the desire to fling myself into her arms.

'It's . . . it's Mimi,' I stammered. 'She's dead.'

'Dead?' Anna was at my side with a speed that belied her size. 'Oh, poor little thing.' She peered over my shoulder. 'Such a beautiful cat, too. She must have picked up poison. There are rats around the canals, you know, and there's poison put down sometimes.'

'No, it isn't poison.' I withdrew the hand I had laid on the cat. As I turned it, palm up, there was a smear of red right across my palm. 'Somebody,' I said tightly, 'has cut Mimi's throat.'

We stared at each other, the horror on her face reflecting my own. Then we heard Jan's voice.

'Oh my!' Anna gasped. 'Jan is coming. He adores that cat. What shall we do?'

'I looked around desperately. There was nowhere in the kitchen to hide the body.

'The window, Anna. We'll have to throw Mimi into the canal.'

It seemed a terrible thing to do, but the truth was far too brutal for Jan to see. We closed the window, and Anna leaned against it with a sigh, her face quite grey.

'Are you all right?' I asked anxiously.

She nodded, and swallowed hard. 'It is just . . . the canal. Poor Mimi, to end up there, like Helen.'

'Like Helen?' My voice rose. 'You don't mean . . . ?'

She nodded, and wiped her eyes on the back of her hand. Clearly the shock of Mimi's death had shaken her, enough for her to spill out the truth.

'They found her in the canal. Suicide.'

There was no time for her to tell me more, because Jan came running in, still in his pyjamas. I had to act normally and take him off to be washed and dressed. It was perhaps, just as well that I had something ordinary to keep me busy. I didn't want to think about what had happened.

Breakfast was an ordeal. There had been no opportunity to tell Jan's parents about what we had found, so I had to sit there, eating croissants, or trying to. Maxime looked at me curiously, and I made an effort to smile and talk naturally. I didn't want her to think that I was brooding over her warning about Hugo. He must have thought me quiet. At one point, our eyes met, he gave me a little encouraging smile. He looked tired, I thought.

Then I felt furious and confused. Why should I feel sorry for him? If anyone deserved sympathy, it was Maxime. She had lost her career, and then to know she had a husband who was playing around. No wonder she had been creating a scene last night.

And yet, when I cast another quick glance at Hugo, I found it hard to believe. He looked pale, and thoroughly weary. He spoke politely to his wife, and smiled at Jan, ruffling the child's hair.

Anna padded in with fresh coffee and to collect the breakfast plates. She, too, looked strained. Apart from little Jan, it occurred to me that the only one of us who seemed normal this morning was Maxime.

'It's your free afternoon today,' she said to me briskly. 'You must make the most of it. What are you going to do?'

I made a brave attempt to bring my mind to bear on what she was saying.

'I think I'll explore the town,' I said. 'It is fascinating. I'd never tire of the canals and the cobbled streets. And those sweet little bridges. It must be rather like Amsterdam, only smaller.'

'Good idea,' she said enthusiastically. 'And the first place you must visit is the Halles Tower. There are the bells to see, of course, but above all, such wonderful views. Have you a camera?'

I shook my head, regretfully. 'I'm afraid not. It's something I must get, but I want a good one.' Six months unemployed had not left me in a position to buy one to my liking. Maxime must have read my thoughts, but was tactful.

'But you must borrow mine,' she suggested. 'Truly, I never use it. When you live in a place, you get used to the sights, you know.'

I was grateful. It would be nice to have some good snaps to send home to Mum and Dad. I had written, of course, but descriptions, and even coloured postcards, are not quite the same.

'Thank you,' I said gratefully. 'That really is very kind of you.'

It almost forced Mimi out of my

mind . . . Almost, but not quite. I had been trying to ignore the truth but it kept creeping into my mind, forcing me to acknowledge it. Whoever had killed Mimi must be in this house!

I picked up my coffee cup, my hand shaking. It was too horrible to contemplate, and yet the facts were quite inescapable. If Mimi had been poisoned, she might have found her way home before dying, but as it was, there was no way she could have moved after receiving that terrible wound. She had been killed right there where she lay in the kitchen.

Suddenly the coffee tasted bitter, and I put down my cup on its saucer in such haste that it clattered. Everyone turned to look at me.

'Sara, are you all right?'

Hugo sounded concerned, but his face was blurred, swimming before me. I felt perspiration breaking out on my forehead, and I pushed back my chair.

'Maxime, could you keep Jan with you please. I don't feel well.'

I didn't wait to hear her reply, but rushed from the room. I couldn't face the kitchen again, and staggered up the stairs on weak legs, reaching my room in time to fling myself on the bed.

There, the nausea gradually passed, and I lay with my eyes closed, trying not to think at all.

'Sara, Sara, what is the matter?'

I sat up at the sound of Hugo's voice, and instinctively turned to him for reassurance. He took hold of me by my shoulders, steadying me.

'It was horrible,' I stammered. 'Horrible!' I shivered and looked down at my hands, even though I had washed them so many times. 'Who would want to kill Mimi? There was blood . . . '

I felt his grasp tighten and then his arms went around me and I found myself weeping against his chest, babbling hysterically about what I had found. I didn't stop to ask what he was doing in my room, whether it was wise, or whether I should tell him to leave. I just clung to him in blind panic.

My hair must have come loose, because he started stroking it, quietening me, making soothing noises, and at last I wept myself calm.

'Hugo, Sara, there you are. Whatever is going on?'

It was only as I heard Maxime's voice that I realised how things must look, and I pulled myself upright, away from Hugo. With shaking hands, I tried to tie back my hair. I felt a fool, and as guilty as could be, although there was nothing to be guilty about. Hugo, however, was quite matter of fact.

'She's had a nasty shock,' he said calmly. 'It seems Mimi has been killed.' He rose to his feet. 'I'd better go down and see about it. Where is Jan?'

I raised my eyes, puffy and hot from crying. My glasses had fallen off my nose on to the bed. 'Oh, don't worry,' I said hurriedly. 'Anna and I disposed of the . . . the . . . in the canal.'

I saw Hugo give his wife a quick glance. Their eyes met, and then Maxime turned to me.

'You poor thing,' she said sympathetically. 'Hugo, you'd better talk to Anna and find out what's happened. I'll stay here with Sara.'

When he hesitated, I gave a watery smile. 'Honestly, I am all right now. It was just all rather upsetting.'

When he had gone, Maxime sat on the bed beside me, and put her arm around my shoulders. 'You mustn't cry any more,' she said gently. 'You're making your eyes red . . . such pretty eyes, too.'

Then she found my glasses. 'Here — oh look, they're all misted up.'

I sat there, numbly, as she picked a tissue from a box on my bedside table and rubbed them.

'There,' she said. 'That should be better. 'Let's see.' She held them up to the light, and then laughed, her green eyes narrowing. 'You're a little fraud, Sara, aren't you? These glasses are a fake.'

It didn't really seem important any more. 'It was the advertisement,' I said matter-of-factly. 'It specifically asked for a plain girl, and I did so want the job.'

'So you deliberately made yourself look a frump!' She held me away from her, searching my face. 'I thought so. You're really a very pretty girl.' She stood up. 'Come along, Sara. Enough of this nonsense. Let's see you as you really are.'

Her voice was teasing, not at all vindictive. I knew she was just trying to cheer me up, but I was glad I didn't have to pretend any more.

'But the advert?'

'Ah well!' She smiled. 'I did have my reasons for that.'

'But I'm sure that Monsieur Rogier . . .'

'*Hugo,*' she said, stressing his name, 'is a very changeable man. I did warn you.'

I stared at her, not understanding. She sighed, and raised her shoulders in a shrug. Then picking up my hairbrush, she deliberately changed the subject. 'Let's see what your hair really looks like.'

I let her play at turning Cinderella

back into a princess. She seemed to be enjoying it. I opened my wardrobe and let her pick out the brightest of my clothes, and I dressed while she watched.

'You have a nice figure,' she said critically. 'And you carry yourself well. But it is the hair that is important. Amazing what a difference it makes. Now that it frames your face, you look quite lovely.'

I smiled, but my heart was heavy. I couldn't help but puzzle over the things she had hinted about Hugo. I found them so hard to believe, and yet I couldn't forget how angry he had been at dinner the night before. What had he said to Jan? Something about getting rid of Mimi?

There was another thing, too. I had noticed it, just as Hugo turned to go out of the room. On his left hand, there was a long, angry, red scratch. Like the scratch you could get from a frightened cat . . .

4

The September sun was bright, but there was a cool bite to the air warning that summer might soon be over. All the same, the sky was blue and the little boats were busy plying their trade up and down the canals. I pulled the zip of my anorak up higher, and leaned over the parapet of the bridge to look down on the water.

Maxime's camera hung around my neck, and now that I had discarded my disguise, I must have looked another typical tourist. I only wished I felt like one. The truth was, I had never been so confused or so frightened in my life. I turned away from the canal and walked slowly towards a café where I sat down, ordered a lemon tea and began to put my thoughts in order.

First, there was Helen, the shadowy figure of the woman who had been employed before me. From the lovelorn girl I had imagined flying back to her boyfriend, she had now emerged as something far more sinister — a body taken from the canal.

I still didn't know the details. I had held back from asking Maxime, and I hadn't seen either Anna or Hugo since morning. I assumed, though, from what Anna had said earlier, that Helen had committed suicide because of a broken heart.

I remembered what little Jan had said about her. 'She laughed a lot.' I sipped my tea, reflecting that it didn't sound much like a girl who was about to fling herself into a canal. What, I wondered, had made the police so sure it was suicide. Couldn't it have been an accident?

But the cat couldn't have cut its throat by accident, I thought with a shudder. I paid for my tea and set off again. The rest of the day was my own, but I couldn't summon up much enthusiasm. There was the museum, of course, and the Beguinage Convent Hugo had told me about. I stood, uncertain, then I remembered Maxime's insistence that I should visit the Halles Tower to see the bells being played.

It was as good a place as any, and might take my mind off these less pleasant matters. I strode briskly along the Wollestraat, forcing myself to appreciate the glowing red of the creeper that covered the wall of one old house, noticing the distinctive stepped roofs, stopping to take a couple of photos. I had nearly reached the market square when I had a strong feeling that I was being followed.

I stopped and turned, pretending to take a snap. Everything seemed quite normal, lots of ordinary sightseers, and a horsedrawn cab clopping along the street. I was becoming obsessed! There was no reason why anybody should follow me. I held the camera up again, and squinted along the street. There was nobody there I knew.

What made me think there would be? Was I expecting to see Hugo perhaps? But why should I? Why should he be there? I muttered to myself, then continued to walk, trying to ignore the peculiar tingle between my shoulder blades.

The flower-sellers were in their usual position under the shady arches, their big green containers crammed with every kind of colourful blooms. There were stands of coloured postcards, too, but I wasn't interested in them today, not now that I had Maxime's camera. I glanced at my watch, and realised I was in time to hear the carillion played on the bells.

It was just as well I was pretty fit. I counted every one of the steps up the tower. There were two hundred and twenty to where the huge Victory Bell was hung, and just over three hundred more to the machine-room which held the massive drum of the automatic mechanism. I was pretty puffed by then. No wonder I seemed to have the place to myself!

To my surprise, it still wasn't time for the bells to begin, and I summoned the energy from somewhere to carry on to the top. I didn't fancy being so close to the forty-seven bronze bells when they all sounded off. My legs felt quite wobbly by then. Maxime was right, though. There was a magnificent view from the top, right across the sharp-pointed roofs, to the spires of churches, and the glint of water, with lines of green trees which I knew bordered the canals. When I managed to get my breath back, I took loads of snaps.

Then the carillion began. I could feel it reverberating under my feet. I would ask Anna when I got back if the tune was a folk song. I stood leaning against the parapet of the tower, the wind tugging at my hair. For a little while, I was completely at ease and happy.

But it didn't last. Too much had happened, too many questions remained unanswered, and not least of those was the one I had been trying not to ask myself. Would it not be sensible to pack my bags and go home?

Part of me knew that it would. The situation here was weird and I knew what my mother would say. On the other hand, I might be getting all worked up over nothing. I had a vivid imagination. Perhaps I imagined the severity of Mimi's wound. But I knew I was just searching for a way out. I'd had to wash the blood off my hands. Of course she could have been in a cat fight, then dragged herself home before dying. That must surely be it.

But what about Hugo's scratched hand? Was that pure coincidence? And his sudden outburst the night before? And Maxime's guarded warnings about him?

I couldn't face any more of the doubts and questions unanswered. I turned and clattered recklessly down the stairs, running away from my thoughts. I didn't give the bells a second glance as I climbed on down. Perhaps that was why I didn't see whoever it was waiting there for me.

All I knew was the unexpected blow in the small of my back after which I was too busy clawing at the wall to look around. My foot missed the next step, my bag and the camera went flying. I was too startled even to cry out as the world spun and the steep stairs rushed up to meet me.

I came to to the sound of foreign voices babbling, and for a moment, I couldn't remember where I was.

'Is she all right?'

'Give her air, everybody.'

'Shall I fetch a doctor?'

I opened my eyes. As I stirred, faces bent over me, concerned.

'I'm all right, really,' I told them as my thoughts came back to me.

'But what happened, mademoiselle?'

I raised a tentative hand to feel the bump rising under my hair. My knees hurt, too, and my side. 'I'm not sure,' I said truthfully. Then added, not so truthfully, 'I must have slipped.'

What could I say? That somebody had pushed me? I didn't even know that for sure myself. I only knew that it had felt as though I received a blow in the back, and that, just for a moment as I fell, I had the impression of a dark figure rushing past me.

Somebody handed me my handbag, and someone else the camera. Stammering my thanks, I scrambled to my feet. Apart from feeling bruised and stiff, I seemed to have escaped without damage.

I walked away, dazed but with my mind made up. I would return to the house and tell Maxime I was leaving. This was too much to be a coincidence. I could no longer tell myself that it was nothing to do with me. I would leave tomorrow.

Then I remembered that I couldn't leave tomorrow. I had promised Jan that I would take him on the boat to Damme, and he had been so looking forward to it. By now, he must have missed Mimi, too, and he had adored his cat. He would be so upset about her disappearance. I couldn't leave him in the lurch.

Perhaps another few days wouldn't matter, if I was careful. But why should anyone attack me? Come to that, why had anyone wanted to kill Helen? I was sure now that was what had happened.

I must have been in a daze, thinking these confused thoughts, because I walked into Hugo without even noticing he was there. He caught me by the arm and steadied me.

'Sara! What on earth are you doing? You look as though you are in a daze.'

I was too shaken to be thinking straight. I stared at him, glad, in spite of myself, that he was there.

'I'm all right,' I stammered.

'What's happened to you?' he demanded.

I was about to tell him I had fallen, but he went straight on. 'Why are you dressed like that? And your hair . . . What's happened to it?' He peered down into my face. 'Where are your glasses?'

It really was the last straw. Here I was, having tumbled halfway down three hundred odd steps and he was mad at me simply because I no longer looked a frump!

'It's a long story,' I said abruptly. 'Maxime knows all about it, and I don't feel like discussing it now. I'm on my way home.'

I pulled away from him and started walking away briskly, conscious of my knees stinging and what felt like a thousand bruises coming up all over my body. He leaped after me, and strode along by my side.

'You have deceived me,' he said curtly. 'I advertised for a plain girl.'

'You didn't complain when I arrived.'

'When you arrived, you didn't look like this!'

'I'm not all that different.'

He caught me by the arm, so that I swung round facing him. 'Stop trying to be so clever. I thought you were too pretty when you came, but I thought maybe you'd be all right. But now you're not pretty, you're damned well beautiful. Why didn't you stay as you were?' He was almost shaking me. 'Why?'

People were glancing at us, but I didn't care, I was so angry. 'Now look here, Monsieur Rogier,' I said angrily, 'I don't feel I owe you any explanations. Your wife doesn't seem to think it matters, and, quite frankly, I don't feel it's very important either.'

I had gained courage through my anger and decided to go on. I took a deep breath. 'Since I came to work for you, I've found a dead cat, discover my predecessor was drowned in the canal and now somebody has just sent me flying down the stairs of the Halles Tower. Well, I've had enough!'

'What did you say?'

One look at my face must have been sufficient, because he put an arm around my shoulders and guided me into the nearest café. I searched desperately in my handbag for a hanky. 'Here,' he said, handing me his. I mopped my eyes and sniffed. By the time he had ordered both of us large brandies, I had pulled myself together.

'Now, suppose you tell me what has

happened,' he demanded.

I told him briefly what had occurred. He listened to me carefully, all the time holding my hand. I don't think he realised he was doing it, but it was comforting just the same. When I had finished, he insisted on examining the bump on my head. 'Are you sure you were pushed?' he asked at last. 'You could have tripped.' He glanced under the table at my feet, clad for the first time since I had been here in fashionable sandals.

'I could have,' I said shortly, 'but I didn't.'

He sipped his brandy, looking at me thoughtfully over the rim of his glass. He was looking incredibly handsome, I thought, annoyed with myself for allowing my feelings to come to the fore.

'You know,' he said, 'this business of the cat has probably upset you more than you think. Then there is learning about Helen.'

'Yes, there is that,' I murmured.

He nodded towards my brandy. 'Drink up,' he ordered. 'It will do you good.'

Obediently I took a sip, and its warmth sent a glow through me.

'You see,' he said. 'Learning about Helen immediately after finding the cat is enough to unsettle anyone. But they really aren't connected.'

'Aren't they?'

He shook his head. 'How could they be? The police investigated thoroughly and were quite satisfied that Helen had committed suicide. It seems she had confided that she was having an unhappy love affair.'

And who was the man involved, I wondered sadly. Did they ever find that out? But I said nothing.

'And Anna thinks perhaps the cat had been fighting.'

I had thought that only minutes ago, but now that he said it, I didn't believe it at all.

'So you see,' he went on, 'when you tripped, it was only natural you should imagine . . .'

Imagine! I hadn't imagined anything, but I just nodded weakly. 'I suppose you're right.'

'Of course I am.' He smiled at me, and the brandy's glow somehow spread right through me. 'You know I . . . we . . . are so glad you came. Jan needed somebody. You have brightened up the whole house.'

'Even though I deceived you?' I couldn't help remarking. 'You don't want me to leave, then?'

For a moment, the smile was wiped off his face, and I could see the lines of strain that somehow made him look older. Then he sighed. 'No,' he said wearily. And then, inexplicably, 'The damage is done now.'

I didn't know what he meant by that, and suddenly I felt tired of the whole thing. I liked him, that was the trouble. I liked him a lot. I liked the way his hair swept back from his broad forehead, the way his lips were firm and turned up at the corners; the way his eyes warmed when he talked about the city he loved.

I liked him far too much.

'I think I'll go back now,' I said. 'I feel in need of a clean-up and a rest. I'm taking Jan to Damme tomorrow.'

He didn't offer to accompany me to the house. I left him and walked wearily back. It hadn't occurred to me to ask him what he was doing, roaming the streets of Bruges once more during normal working hours. That was twice he had just happened to be around.

I wished I hadn't told him about my plans for the next day, and I wished I hadn't been as aware of his dark suit. Whoever had rushed past me on those narrow stairs had been wearing something dark.

* * *

Anna was busy baking when I got back, and Jan was with her, making gingerbread men.

'Madame had a migraine,' she explained in answer to my unspoken question. 'So the little one has been helping me today, haven't you, my sweet?'

He nodded, serious. 'Because Mimi has left,' he said in a sad voice. 'Anna says she had to go, because her family wanted her. I expect it was the same with Helen, don't you?'

He looked up at me with such trusting eyes, I felt my throat constrict. 'Yes, something like that, my dear.' I couldn't help putting my arms around him and giving him a hug. 'Don't you think you'd better run off and wash those hands? You're covered in flour.'

When he had gone, I asked Anna something that had been bothering me.

'Anna, when they found Helen, what did the police doctor discover?' She gave me a suspicious look and I found myself going hot with embarrassment. 'I'm not being ghoulish. I just want to know.'

Anna turned to slide a last batch of cakes into the oven. 'She wasn't pregnant, if that's what you're getting at,' she said disapprovingly. 'They simply said it was death by drowning.'

'And that was all?'

Her eyebrows shot up. 'Wasn't that enough? There had been a blow on the head, but they thought that could have been a boat.'

I closed my eyes at the horrible picture that conjured up, but I pressed on. 'And where was she supposed to have jumped from?'

I don't really know why I asked that, and a moment later I was wishing I hadn't.

'From your bedroom,' she said reluctantly. 'They found the window open. She must have thrown herself out.'

5

I felt quite on edge as I went back upstairs to my room. As I opened the door and entered the bright bedroom, I couldn't help wondering if it had really housed a girl so desperate that she would commit suicide. I looked around at the old-fashioned flowery wallpaper, the heavy, polished furniture.

Was it true that people left their imprint on a house where they had been desperately unhappy? I closed my eyes, and tried to sense Helen's presence, but there was nothing. As I opened them I felt rather silly.

It was a pleasant room; no ghosts lingered here. I moved over to the window, and pulled up the bottom half. It opened on a level with my shoulders. It should have gone higher, but it stuck there. It would not have been easy to jump out. Helen would have had to crouch on the window-sill, I reflected, balancing there before plunging into the canal. Or perhaps she had dived out, head first.

I leaned out of the window, looking down at the water that had so charmed me before. Somehow the waters had lost all their appeal. I retreated hastily into the room. Anyone coming quietly behind me could have tipped me up, and over I would have gone. Not that it would have killed me if they did, because I could swim.

Had Helen been a swimmer? If her attacker did not know that, pushing her into the canal would be a risky thing to try. But there was the bump on her head. Suppose it wasn't caused by a boat. Suppose somebody had crept up and hit her?

Oh, this was ridiculous! I closed the window, and went to lie down on the bed. I suppose I ought to go and ask how Maxime was, and explain about the mishap with the camera. I did hope it wasn't damaged in any way. I raised myself off the bed, and left my room, climbing the stairs to Maxime's.

'Entrez,' a voice called when I knocked.

It was dark in the room. She had closed the wooden shutters over the windows, but I could just make out the bed.

'Maxime, I'm sorry you have a migraine. Is there anything I can do now?'

'Oh, Sara, is that you?' There was a movement from the bed. 'Will you open the shutters, just a little. Thanks.'

I did as she asked, and when I turned back to her, I found her sitting up. She must have been lying on top of the bed with a dressing-gown over her. For she was now arranging it over her legs.

'Are you feeling any better?'

She sighed. 'Yes, it has begun to improve. I really think I might come down for dinner.' She pressed a graceful hand against her forehead. 'Such a nuisance, and I was looking forward to spending the day with Jan.'

'He's been helping Anna to bake,' I told her. 'He's been quite happy.'

She made a petulant sound. 'Oh, I'm sure he'd rather be with Anna, or with you, than with his poor mother.'

Then she chuckled, and patted the bed. 'Don't mind me, my dear. I'm just feeling sorry for myself. Come and sit here. Tell me all about your day. Did you have a nice time?'

I decided on a version of the truth. 'Yes, I did, until I tumbled stupidly halfway down the steps of the Halles.'

She sat bolt upright at that, and then winced and leaned back.

'But my dear, are you all right?'

'Oh, yes,' I said hastily. 'Don't worry about me. But I'm afraid the camera went flying. I don't *think* it's damaged, but perhaps I ought to take it to someone to find out. If it is I will pay, of course.'

'Don't you dare think of it. I never use it, anyway. *You* are more important.' Then, strangely, she put her hand on my wrist. It felt cold against my skin.

'Did you see anybody there?' she asked urgently.

'How d'you mean? I didn't see anybody at the tower.' I decided honestly was the best policy. 'I did bump into Hugo later. He very kindly bought me a brandy.'

'Ah . . . ' Her sigh sounded almost satisfied. 'And you're still sure your fall was an accident?'

'You're not suggesting . . . '

'That it was my husband?' Her grip grew tighter. 'I don't know. I only know he frightens me.'

'But Maxime, you can't mean that.'

'Oh, can't I?' She was talking fast now, her voice low and vindictive. 'You don't know what he is really like. He hates me, do you know that?'

'But, he seems so nice.'

'Well, of course he does!' She rose up in the bed and leaned closer to me, her lips close to my ear. 'But who was paying attention to Helen, laughing and joking with her? And then Helen dies. Who said he would get rid of the cat?

And then the cat dies. And could he be following you about?'

I could feel goose pimples breaking out on my skin. Her words held a queer kind of logic and yet it was quite unbelievable.

'But why should he hate you, his own wife?'

She glanced at the door nervously. 'He didn't like my career. I could have carried on, you know, once I was better after having Jan. But Hugo wouldn't hear of it. He didn't like my being on the stage with other men staring at me.' She looked at me with a strange kind of regret in her eyes. 'He hates anything beautiful. I shouldn't have encouraged you, Sara. I should have left you as you were. You were safer then.'

I shook my head in a daze. Every moment was taking me deeper and deeper into a maze of suspicion and fear, and still I couldn't believe all this of Hugo.

'I think I'd better go now, Maxime,' I stammered. 'I want to have a shower before dinner. And tidy my room a little.'

'You will think about what I have said,' she said urgently. 'Perhaps it would be better if you left here.'

I had thought the very same thing!

'I can't go yet,' I answered. 'I promised Jan that we would go by boat to Damme tomorrow.'

She relaxed. 'You should be safe enough there,' she said. 'So long as you are with Jan.'

On the way back to my room, I met Anna with Jan. She had on her black coat and hat.

'Sara, I know it's your day off, but could you watch over Jan for a little while. I want to pop out to the shops.'

'No, of course I don't mind,' I said quickly. 'Why didn't you tell me you needed something? I could have gone to the shops for you.'

'Well, I didn't know then, did I?' She shook her head at me and grinned. 'It's only that I've run out of flour. I did so much baking, and now I don't have enough for the apple pie for this evening.' As she left us, she called back over her shoulder, 'It's Mr Hugo's favourite.'

'Maxime should be down for dinner, too,' I called after her.

For a moment, she stopped and I could have sworn she grimaced with displeasure. Then she was gone.

'Come along, Jan,' I said. 'Let's play cards for a while. Can you play snap?'

'I can.' He smiled mischievously. 'And I can beat you, too.'

As we sat at the kitchen table, playing, my mind kept wandering.

'Snap! I've won, I've won.' Jan was bouncing up and down with excitement, bringing me back to the present.

'So you have.' I smiled. I hadn't been concentrating on the game, indulging in silly speculations. 'Come on now, we have to get ready for dinner.'

★ ★ ★

Next morning, it promised to be yet another fine day. It was a little misty when I awoke, but by breakfast, the weather was clearing.

I avoided seeing Hugo by having toast and coffee in the kitchen with Anna, on the pretext of getting breakfast over early. I didn't want to see him. I felt sure he would be able to read in my eyes all the doubts that Maxime had put into my head.

Jan sat up at the big kitchen table, too, happy to be eating his cereal, chatting excitedly about going on the boat. I was glad to see that he didn't appear to be missing Mimi as much as I had expected. When he had finished breakfast, I dressed him then ran upstairs to fetch my own jacket.

'You're looking very pretty these days,' Anna said.

I looked at her sharply, but there was nothing but approval on her broad features.

'It suits you, your hair loose like that,' she went on with a smile. 'Young people should look nice. Be bright. Cheer the place up a bit. I have packed you a lunch.' She held out a basket, its contents covered by a white linen napkin.

I muttered my thanks and kissed her cheek, then I slipped on my anorak, put my purse in my pocket, and picked up the bag.

'Are you quite ready?' I asked Jan. He was hopping from one foot to the other with impatience. I held out my other hand. 'Come along then, let's be on our way.'

Maxime waylaid us in the hallway, dramatic in a pale silver-grey suit with a white collar.

'So you are off to enjoy yourselves?' With a graceful, fluid movement, she kneeled beside Jan and gathered him to her. 'Wouldn't you rather stay with your mother today, darling?' she crooned.

'No!' he replied sharply, wriggling out of her grasp and running to me. 'I want to go with Sara.'

Maxime spread out her arms dolefully. 'You see?'

I could feel my face becoming hot.

Sorry though I was for her, there were times when she made me feel quite uncomfortable.

'You could come, too, Maxime. Jan would really like that.'

She shrugged. 'I have no wish to ride on a boat with a cold wind blowing my hair. It would bring on another migraine. No, off you go without me.'

I didn't press her any further, but hurried Jan out of the house. I could understand Hugo's wish to employ a nanny for Jan. Maxime's rather possessive mother love did not create a very healthy atmosphere for the child.

We caught a bus to the quay where the boat we were to join was moored. The vessel was bright, white-painted with colourful flags flying from its mast. We crossed the narrow gang-plank, then went on to the open top deck and took our seats.

There were already quite a few passengers aboard, and no doubt even more down below, inside.

There was a stiff breeze blowing so I

pulled Jan close against me to help shield him. Not that he would have noticed the cold, he was too busy looking over the side.

We cast off and I settled down to enjoy myself. This was to be a day when I could leave all my doubts and fears behind. All that mattered was the progress of the boat through the water, past the tall trees that lined both sides of the canal like sentinels. Autumn was on its way, painting the landscape with vivid hues. Never had a sky looked so blue, contrasted against a white wind-mill in the distance.

'There's people canoeing,' Jan said, standing to get a better view. I held on to his coat.

'Be careful.' I turned at the sound of a well-known voice. 'I don't want to lose you, son.'

'Papa!' Jan's face was a picture. I dare say mine was, too, but for different reasons.

'What are you doing here?' I exclaimed. 'You didn't say you were coming.'

'Didn't I?' One eyebrow rose in amusement. 'It was, shall we say, a spur-of-the-moment decision. May I sit here?' I edged up, and he sat between us.

'You're coming with us, Papa? All the way to Damme?'

Hugo gave me a steady look. 'If Miss Sara will allow.'

I blushed. 'It's not for me to say,' I muttered. 'But if you were to be going, there was really no need for me to be here.'

'Nonsense. We need you, to keep us in order.' He ruffled Jan's hair. 'What d'you say, Jan?'

There was nothing I could do about it. Hugo must have already been down below when we came on board, lying in wait. My heart missed a beat. What was it Maxime had said about being safe so long as I was with Jan?

'Are you listening to me, Sara?'

I came to earth with a bump, to find Hugo looking at me quizzically. 'I'm . . . I'm sorry, Hugo. I was miles away.

What were you saying.'

'I was telling Jan that Napoleon's men built this canal. Can you imagine it, poor devils, slaving away to make this, just for our delight today?'

'Did he know we were coming, Papa?' Jan asked, wide-eyed, and we both laughed.

That laughter broke the ice. I refused to consider that there could be any sinister motive behind Hugo's presence here today. What could be more natural than that a man should want to take a boat trip with his son? If a small voice insisted on asking why he had not told Maxime he was coming, then that small voice was firmly silenced.

He was talking to Jan now, his head turned away from me, so I could study him without his noticing. The wind was ruffling his hair, just as it was blowing mine across my face. I could see the clean curve of his jaw, the deepening of a laughter line as he smiled at his son.

Then he turned and smiled at me, and as I smiled back, I had a crazy desire to tuck my arm through his and lean against him, cuddled up to him just as Jan was.

I knew now why I had decided to stay here in Bruges. I knew why I had ignored Maxime's warnings and refused to believe the things she had said about her husband. Commonsense told me that the evidence was stacking up against him, but I had ignored it persistently. Now I knew why.

Against all my instincts, indeed, against all commonsense, I was falling headlong in love with Hugo Rogier.

6

'Papa, how did the men build the canal? Wasn't it hard, with all this water in it? Did they wear diving suits?'

It was just as well Hugo was bending over Jan, answering the child's never-ending questions. It gave me time to compose myself, calm the ridiculous pounding of my heart and get a grip on myself.

I stared at a woman sitting opposite, not really seeing her until she moved suddenly and, realising how rude I must seem, I flushed and turned away. At least the shock of admitting the strength of my feelings had answered the question of whether I should stay or leave.

Tomorrow, I had to hand in my notice, and then I would pack, and put Belgium behind me for ever. With it, I knew I had to put aside all thoughts of

Hugo Rogier, however much that hurt.

But not today, I told myself, clutching pitifully at that small crumb of comfort . . . no, not today.

The boat ploughed steadily along, the throbbing of its engines pulsating through the decks to the soles of my feet. On the canal banks the trees were still planted at regular intervals, but now, beyond them, I could see green fields and the occasional windmill. A stiff breeze blew, tugging at my hair and making me turn the collar of my jacket higher.

Hugo noticed immediately. Even though he was engrossed with his son, he appeared to be as aware of me as I was of him, or was that just wishful thinking on my part?

'Are you cold, Sara?'

As I shook my head, he took my hands, clasping them in his. His fingers were warm and strong.

'You're frozen, you poor thing,' he said with quick sympathy. 'Would you like to go below decks?'

With an effort, I found my voice. 'No, really. It's lovely up here, and besides, Jan is enjoying it so much.'

I could have added that I didn't want to move, because if I did he would take away his hands, and I wanted to stay for ever as we were. There were other passengers packed closely around us, but as far as I was concerned, they might never have existed. I was with Hugo, and that was enough.

I had the sense to know that I mustn't risk him seeing how I felt, so I turned and stared over his shoulder across the stern of the boat, as though fascinated in the creamy wake we were leaving behind.

'Tell us more,' I said firmly, 'about Napoleon and how he built the canal.'

He did, but I wasn't really listening. I was too busy absorbing everything about him, the breadth of his shoulders, the pressure of his fingers where they closed on mine, the sound of his voice, so deep and with its delicious accent.

The way I felt had hit me badly, and

I wasn't sure how to cope. Nothing so strong had ever happened to me before. I had always imagined that falling in love would be an exciting, happy experience. This was, in a strange and wonderful way, but what I hadn't been prepared for was the pain that came with it.

The trip to Damme was all too short for me. Soon we arrived at the little jetty and I had to move with the other travellers, following Hugo and Jan on to dry land. They stepped off first, and stood waiting for me.

'We're going to enjoy ourselves,' Hugo said with a grin, and a dare-devil glint in his eye. 'We're going to make this the best day ever, aren't we, Jan?'

As Jan piped out his excited agreement, I stepped off the jetty. Hugo caught hold of me to steady me, and it felt quite natural that we should remain like that, his arm tucked through mine. We all stepped out together, laughing. This was a day I was to cherish and I was determined to make the most of it.

There wasn't a great deal to do in Damme. It was a very small town, with a large, steep-roofed town hall dominating the central square. We walked around the square once, looking in shop windows and pointing out to Jan the things of interest. From there, we then walked along the path edging the canal. In the warmth of the sun, we sat down on a grassy bank to watch a man fishing.

'Why bother to build a canal to this place?' I asked. 'I mean, it's lovely, unspoiled and peaceful, but it's so quiet.'

Hugo lay back, his hands behind his head. 'Ah, but it wasn't always like this. Bruges and Damme were once busy and prosperous, mainly with the cloth trade.'

'If I lived here,' Jan said, 'I would have a boat to sail in.'

'That's a fine idea,' his father agreed. I detected a hint of sadness, but why should a man like Hugo be sad? He had everything, a good business, money, an adorable son and a beautiful wife.

I decided that it might be better not to ask questions like that.

'Is anyone hungry?' I asked brightly. 'Anna has packed this basket, and judging by the weight, there is plenty for three.'

'Not now,' Hugo said. 'Later.' He scrambled to his feet, and, grabbing my hand, hauled me up. 'Come along, you two. I will introduce you to one of the gastronomic delights of Damme.'

'What's that, Papa. What's a 'nomic delight?'

I wanted to know, too, but Hugo just laughed and told us both to wait and see. As we made our way back towards the town, Jan walked beside me, his tiny hand in mine, and I thought ruefully that anybody seeing us would take us for a happy, united family.

'Here we are.' Hugo's voice broke into my dreams.

We had arrived at a restaurant, and Hugo soon found us a table near the window, where we could still look out on the mirror-calm waters of the canal. He spoke to the waitress in Flemish, so that I had no idea what to expect until she returned with plates piled high with waffles.

'Waffles!' I laughed. 'I thought they were an American speciality.'

'Good heavens, no! This is the place to find the real thing.'

Truly I had never seen such a huge waffle as the one on my plate, golden and crisp, and with little holes each of which housed a different portion of fruit. The whole thing was drenched in caster sugar and topped with cream.

Jan was digging in to his with every sign of enjoyment.

'Hang on, I'll cut it up for you,' I said.

When I eventually tasted mine, I turned to Hugo in surprise. 'There's liqueur in this!'

'D'you know,' he said slowly, 'when you do that, you look just like Jan, all eyes and a sticky mouth.'

I looked at his son, who was busy

tucking in. 'Surely . . . '

Hugo laughed. 'Don't worry, Jan's is non-alcoholic, and it won't hurt him to indulge, for once.'

There was a touch of cynicism in his voice that made me wonder, but he carried on. 'Do you enjoy yours?'

Like Jan, I was too busy eating to talk until I had finished! I leaned back with a sigh of satisfaction, looking down at my sticky hands.

'Here.' Hugo took out his handkerchief and began to wipe my fingers with gentle concentration. When he had done that to his satisfaction he put a hand under my chin and wiped the corners of my mouth. Our eyes met and his face was suddenly serious.

I drew away from him. 'You'd . . . you'd better do the same for Jan,' I gabbled breathlessly. 'He's in a worse state, by far.'

Without a word, he wiped Jan's mouth. 'I think we'll catch the next boat back,' he said abruptly. 'We've seen all there is to see in Damme, and Jan is really only interested in the boat ride.'

It was as though he wanted to be rid of me as soon as he could. Had I been so transparent?

'Yes,' I agreed. 'Of course.'

He should never have come, I told myself angrily. If only he had left us alone. I could have stifled my feelings, knowing he belonged to another woman, knowing he could be nothing to me. Why had he decided to join us on our excursion?

All the way back, I wondered that. We hardly spoke to one another, so I had plenty of time to ponder. Why had Hugo Rogier been following us about, and why had he appeared as if by magic on the boat today? The answer would have been obvious if he had flirted with me, if he had by any look or gesture shown that he was interested. But quite the contrary. When our eyes had met in that unguarded moment, he had backed away as if stung.

So what did he want? All my confusion, doubts and fears returned. I couldn't help remembering Maxime's warnings, even though I found it hard to imagine they could possibly have any truth in them. I sat rigidly by Hugo's side, trying to ignore him. I thought about everything that had happened in the Rogier household.

A girl had died, a girl who had supposedly thrown herself from my bedroom window because she was unhappy. But she'd been a girl Jan said had laughed a lot. Now a cat had died and somebody had attacked me. There had to be some connection between these events, but I couldn't think of one, except, perhaps, Hugo Rogier.

I closed my eyes. It was all too much for me. I might think these things about Hugo, but the moment I looked at him, my heart told me that it was all nonsense, no matter what Maxime had said.

'We're nearly back at Bruges,' I said with some regret. 'What about this lunch Anna has packed? Jan must be hungry now, even in spite of the waffle.'

It was the first time I had really spoken directly to Hugo since we had left Damme, and at first he seemed to tighten up and avoid my gaze. Then he gave a sigh and looked me straight in the eyes.

'We'll have a picnic,' he said. 'I know just the place.'

It was called the Minnewater. Huge trees gave shade from the sun and shelter from the breeze and we managed to find a quiet spot on the sloping stretch of grass near to the edge of the lake. The setting could not have been more idyllic — or more romantic.

But I was on my guard now, and determined to be practical and down-to-earth. I concentrated on examining Anna's offerings. As I had expected, there was ample for three, especially after what we had already eaten.

'Have a sandwich first, Jan,' I advised. 'There's egg and cress or cream cheese with celery.'

Hugo was already diving in. 'She's packed my favourites.'

There were also biscuits, little iced cakes, fruit and a flask of home-made lemonade to quench our thirst. When he had eaten enough, Jan took the crusts down to the water to feed the swans.

Alone for the first time with Hugo, I was too aware of him to be comfortable.

'It's beautiful here,' I said at last.

'D'you know what Minnewater means?'

I looked at him, interested. 'No, tell me.'

His gaze was steady. 'It means Lake of Love.'

'Oh!' I could feel my colour rising. 'Bruges is so picturesque,' I babbled. 'Everywhere you go, it's like a picture postcard. I should have brought the camera.' I hesitated. 'I should have taken some photos, to remind me, when I leave.'

He didn't say anything at first, but I could feel his stillness. 'You're leaving?' he said eventually.

I nodded vigorously. 'I think it best,' I said. 'Too much has been happening.'

'But it has nothing to do with you!'

'Hasn't it?' I raised my eyes to his. 'How do I know that?' I said slowly. 'How do I know I won't end up in the canal, like Helen? Maxime thinks . . .'

'Ah!' He nodded, and his mouth twisted. 'I might have guessed Maxime had something to do with this. What has she been saying to you?'

'Nothing,' I said defensively. 'Look, is Jan all right there?'

I made to rise, but he pulled me back roughly. 'Sara, I've got to talk to you. Leave Jan alone, he's happy enough.'

'But . . .'

'Please! I have to talk to someone.'

I couldn't ignore the plea, so I remained seated on the grass, staring out over the lake rather than look at Hugo.

He began hesitantly at first. 'You should have seen Maxime when I first met her in Paris. She was magnificent. I was sure I was in love.' There was a pause. 'I was in love.'

There was a long silence. I couldn't

bear it, picturing it, seeing her through his eyes.

'Go on,' I said.

He drew in breath. 'I was crazy about her, I suppose. Perhaps I wasn't fair. I didn't realise how much her career meant to her.'

As he talked, I could see it all, the ambitious young woman at the height of her career, flattered and swept off her feet by such an ardent pursuer. It had been a charmed time, he told me, full of parties and dances and Maxime's friends. They had wined and dined, gone to the theatre, the opera. And at last, she had agreed to marry him. And that was when reality crept in.

'I could understand,' he said carefully, 'that she would not want to be tied down to domesticity here. But Bruges was my home, my business. I had to return some time. So she came with me.'

It had been a mistake. Maxime had been terribly unhappy, and finally, Hugo had decided that they must sell up and move back to Paris, if he wanted to save his marriage. But fate intervened when Maxime became pregnant.

'We both wanted a family but we hadn't planned it to happen so soon,' Hugo explained.

'So, you were happy about it?'

His smile was a wry one. 'I was ecstatic, but Maxime hated the idea. It put an end to all her plans. There was no way she could return to opera once she was pregnant. She resented the pregnancy all the way. Perhaps that was why she had such a bad time.'

Anna had hinted as much to me. 'She was ill afterwards, wasn't she?' I prompted.

He gave a short laugh. 'That is putting it delicately.' He saw my puzzled expression. 'Yes, she was ill. She had a nervous breakdown. The specialist said there was no way she could handle the strain of a career again. I would have to be very careful of her.'

But loving her so much, surely he

had not minded that? His next words reassured me.

'I would have done anything for her. I was so happy, to have her, to have my son, but she blamed me for the birth. She blamed me for the end of her career. She still does. Maxime hates me.'

He looked tired, despondent, I longed to hold him, but I had to keep myself aloof, remembering Maxime's words . . . 'He hates me . . . d'you know that?' Which one of them was I to believe?

'Hugo, why are you telling me this?' I asked softly.

But before he could reply, Jan came running up, and we had to stop talking. I rummaged around in the basket to find some more crumbs, and Jan went off with a bag full.

'I tell you,' Hugo continued, 'so that you can understand why there is sometimes an atmosphere in the house.' He looked across to where Jan was so happily occupied, and his eyes softened.

'I wanted Jan to be happy, to have someone around who was young, carefree, relaxed. That's why I advertised for a nanny.'

I could understand that. I had been doubtful myself of Maxime's attitude toward her son, ignoring him one moment and possessively demonstrative the next. But obviously, having Helen in the house hadn't helped matters.

'But Helen was not the cheerful girl you had thought?' I asked.

'It appears not. She was unhappy about some man.'

A thought was hovering at the edge of my mind. 'How did the police find out about that?'

He shrugged. 'I believe Maxime told them. Helen had confided in her. They were quite friendly for a while.'

'Was Maxime jealous of Helen?'

'Of course not!'

His reply was too vehement, too ready. Perhaps my doubt showed in my face, because he rubbed a hand across his eyes as if tired, before continuing.

'There may be a moment in time when we do something foolish. A thing we later wish we could undo — but can't. I married Maxime.'

He looked at me, and between us there were words unspoken, but which I understood well enough.

'She is still my wife,' he went on quietly, 'and she is Jan's mother. I would not, could not betray that, even if I wanted to.'

That was his answer to what he had read in my eyes. I had known instinctively that that was how it would be, and I wouldn't have wanted it to be any different. Any other answer and I could not have loved him so. Hugo cleared his throat. 'So you see,' he went on, 'why Maxime might say things to you. But all this has nothing to do with poor Mimi or with you falling down the tower stairs, or even with Helen's death.'

I could see he really believed that. He would not allow himself to entertain the idea that it could be anything else but coincidence. Perhaps he was right, but it really didn't seem to matter any more.

'I still think I should go away, Hugo.'

This time, he did not pretend to misunderstand me. He stroked my hair away from my face and ran his fingers gently down my cheek.

'Sweet Sara. You've brought sunshine into our lives . . . mine and Jan's.' He smiled sadly. 'Even when you were wearing those dreadful old specs and those terrible clothes.'

Suddenly, he took my hand and raised it to his lips. His head bent over and I longed to stroke his hair, to make some gesture of reassurance, of love, but for both our sakes, I stayed still.

Then he dropped my hand. 'You're quite right. It would perhaps be better if you were to leave.'

As if filled by an uncontrollable urge to rid himself of his feelings, he jumped to his feet and called to Jan.

'Come along, old man. Time you were going home.'

He turned to me, formal and polite. 'D'you mind if I drop you near the house? I have to call in at the office before returning.'

'That will be quite all right,' I returned, equally polite.

But our eyes were saying something so completely different.

7

'Thank you for bringing us home. And, thank you for a lovely day.'

Hugo had brought us in the car to the corner of the Quai Vert.

'This has been a day I shall always remember,' he said softly. He reached out of the open window of the car and touched my hand. 'Thank you, Sara,' he murmured.

The blood rushed to my face, and I stood staring after him as he drove away. Then I was left to escort Jan back to the house, which seemed darker and more menacing than ever.

Jan couldn't wait to run to Anna to tell her about his day, and as I sat by the kitchen table drinking a welcome cup of tea, watching the two of them, it was obvious to me that there was no way we could keep quiet about Hugo having been with us.

Jan was full of it, bouncing around and chattering non-stop. Clearly his father's presence on our trip had made his day. I only hoped that Maxime would not object, or jump to the wrong conclusions.

'You enjoyed yourself, so much is obvious. That is good.' Anna poured out another cup for herself. 'And Monsieur Hugo, it will have done him good. He has been looking very tense.'

I merely nodded. 'And Jan enjoyed it, too.'

'So you had lovely time, my little pet,' she chortled, hugging Jan. 'I feel envious, but never mind. Look mon petit, I have made another batch of gingerbread men.'

'He'll never eat his dinner,' I pointed out. 'You should have seen what he has tucked away.'

She just laughed. 'So long as he is happy.'

'Oh, I'm sure he has been happy.'

We both turned as a sneering voice broke into our conversation. Maxime stood in the kitchen doorway. Jan shrank closer to me, burying his head against my side.

'What a touching sight!' she mocked, folding her arms and leaning back against the door post.

She had changed into a long black gown, stark in its simplicity, and she was wearing more make-up than usual. Her cheeks were highlighted with bright patches of colour, and her eyes, skilfully outlined, were glittering green.

'My dear son would much rather be with you, Sara. But then, so would my darling husband, isn't that so?'

My heart lurched. Obviously she knew that Hugo had been with us, and she resented the fact. It was understandable enough, I only hoped that I could put her mind at rest. I prised Jan's fingers from my jacket and pushed him towards Anna.

'Go and have your gingerbread man, Jan. I want to talk to Mummy.' I straightened up and gave Maxime a nervous smile. 'But not here, I think.'

She laughed mockingly. 'Oh, indeed not. Not in front of the children, eh? How terribly British of you.'

She swept ahead of me into the drawing-room. I followed her, closing the door behind me.

'I don't know what you're thinking, Maxime, but I can assure you . . . ' I began but got no further.

She whirled around, pointing an accusing finger. 'Thinking! I'll tell you what I'm thinking, you prissy little English miss. I'm thinking that you are nothing but a man-eating little slut.'

I bit back the anger that was beginning to rise in me. I understood how Maxime must feel. She was possessive and jealous, unsure of herself, trapped in a marriage which was not to her liking, but which she would defend to the death. All the same, I was no danger to her, if only I could convince her of that.

'If you would just calm down,' I said gently. 'And tell me what I have done that is so terrible. You will bring on another migraine if you upset yourself like this.'

'And whose fault would that be?' She flung herself into a low armchair, glaring up at me. All the same, she seemed a little less fraught, and I ventured to press home my advantage.

'Tell me, Maxime, just what has upset you?'

She stared at me through narrowed eyes without speaking, but I stood my ground and met her gaze.

'Very well,' she spat out at last. 'I rang my husband's office to speak with him, and I was told he had taken a day off. He had gone — so they informed me — on a boat trip to Damme!'

She looked me up and down scornfully. 'Do you deny that?'

'No,' I said calmly. 'Why should I?'

'Really!' She sat upright in her chair. 'Of all the brazen . . . '

'Your husband, Madame,' I continued steadily, 'decided that he would like a day out with his son. That was a perfectly natural thing to do. When Jan and I got on the boat, Monsieur Rogier was already on board. I knew nothing about it.'

'As if I believe that!'

'I can assure you it's true.' I tried a smile. 'Really, Maxime, you can't possibly imagine that Monsieur Rogier is interested in me.'

She jumped to her feet and began pacing the room. She was holding a handkerchief between her hands, picking at it nervously. That, more than anything, warned me that she was in a highly-nervous state. This was not the woman who had been so charming to me, so eager that I should show myself off to the best advantage. She had changed completely.

I must try to calm her down, or she would be ill again, and it would be all my fault. I had to try to placate her, for Hugo's sake.

'Maxime,' I urged, 'you have no need to worry about me. Your husband loves you.'

'No!' She rounded on me then, and

there was something in her eyes that halted me in my tracks. 'He hates me. You have made him hate me.'

'That's nonsense. Please listen to me!'

'I should have known. I should have seen through you, with your dowdy clothes and your silly spectacles that you didn't need at all, and your ugly flat shoes.'

'But I've explained all that. It was because of the advertisement. I thought you understood.'

'Understood!' Her laughter was high and wild. 'Yes, I understood all right. I'm not blind! I know a pretty girl when I see one. It was all part of your plan.'

I was beginning to feel desperate. I just wasn't getting through to her at all.

'But Maxime,' I pleaded, 'it was you who insisted I let my hair down, and dressed in smarter clothes. It was you . . . '

'Ah, yes.' She stood still for a moment, looking at me slyly. 'That was clever of me, wasn't it? That showed you that I was not to be fooled.'

'I wasn't trying to fool anybody,' I urged. 'Only to keep the job I wanted.'

'Naturally. And why did you want it? To find yourself a rich man. So you decided to steal mine.'

She almost spat the words out. It was no use. She seemed quite beside herself, and I realised there was only one thing to do.

'I don't think this is getting us anywhere,' I said, trying to sound firm and unconcerned. 'I was going to tell you today, in any case. I'm handing in my notice, Maxime. I'm going home to England.'

If I thought that would stop her, I couldn't have been more wrong. It seemed as though I had only thrown more fuel on the fire.

'You *dare* to hand in your notice,' she shrieked. 'As if . . . as if you were dismissing *me*. How dare you!'

My patience was beginning to wear thin. Ill or not, Maxime was going too far. I couldn't stand there and take any more.

'Well, what do you want?' I snapped. 'I would have thought you'd be glad to see the back of me.'

'I want to know the truth,' she shouted. 'And you're going to tell me. How far has this gone? How many times have you sneaked out to meet Hugo?' She stalked up to me, until she was standing only inches away from me, her eyes holding mine with a fixed stare.

'And at night. Has he been creeping about?'

'That's enough,' I cried, now furious. 'You don't know what you're saying. You're out of your mind.'

The stinging slap across my cheek came so swiftly that I couldn't escape it. I just gasped and staggered back, staring at her.

'Don't you dare call me mad,' she whispered. 'Nobody must ever dare to say that.'

With a sob, I turned and fled.

'Come back here! I haven't finished with you!' she shouted from the foot of the stairs, but I ignored her and ran upstairs to my room.

I ran cold water into the basin, and splashed handfuls of it on to my burning cheek. Then I patted my face dry, and made myself sit down and take several deep breaths.

I was still trembling. I had known Maxime was neurotic, but I had never imagined she could behave in this way. Was this how she had been with Hugo that night when Anna and I had stood listening? And had she shown this side of her character to Helen? Perhaps that was why the poor girl had been depressed.

The niggling little thought that had come to me while I had been with Hugo by the lake returned. Who had actually told the police that Helen was upset over a boyfriend? It could have been only Maxime. How did they know that was the truth? Perhaps Helen had fallen in love with Hugo, even as I had done, and perhaps Maxime had taunted her to the point of despair. All I knew was that it couldn't have been Hugo's fault.

I rose and dragged my cases out of the wardrobe. I would take the first train to Ostend and catch the boat back to England. I hadn't wanted to leave like this. I had hoped to leave with some dignity, on friendly terms with Maxime, never letting her guess my feelings for Hugo.

What made it more difficult was that, deep in my heart, I did feel some guilt about all the things Maxime had accused me of. But I'd done nothing deliberately, I told myself desperately. I had not meant to fall in love with Hugo, and no one would ever know.

And what about Hugo? I didn't believe he was in love with me, but he had indicated he was attracted. He was a very unhappy man, I knew. Who could blame him if for just one moment, he had felt something that was fresh, sweet and wonderful.

Yet he had done no wrong. He would never leave Maxime, never destroy the bonds of his marriage, no matter what it cost him. Why couldn't Maxime see that? If only she knew how loyal he was, perhaps she would not be so jealous.

I had to pack straight away. Perhaps I would even be gone before Hugo returned. It would be better that way. I rubbed a hand across my eyes. I would miss Jan, too. He had won my heart. What would happen to him, passed from one nanny to another? Or would Maxime pack him off to boarding school as soon as she was able? My heart ached for him.

A tap at the door interrupted my thoughts, and I froze.

'Who is it?' I asked.

The door opened and Maxime slid into my room. In contrast to my own dishevelled appearance, her hair was still a sleek, shining cap, her make-up perfect. I turned my back on her, and threw some underwear into a case.

'I don't think there's any more to say,' I said tersely. 'I'd rather you left me alone, Maxime.'

'Are you telling me to get out of one of my own rooms, in my own house?'

She sounded icy calm now, amused even. I cast her a suspicious glance, but she only smiled enigmatically. Perhaps she had come to her senses.

'No, of course not,' I muttered. 'But as you can see, I'm busy.'

'Don't let me stop you.'

She wandered around my room, touching this, picking up that. She fingered the two blue vases that stood upon the mantelpiece, straightened a picture, ran her hands over the bronze figure of a mother and child that stood on the table beside the window.

Perhaps she was making sure I hadn't stolen anything. In her present frame of mind, I wouldn't have been surprised if she had accused me of such a thing. I decided to have one last try at clearing myself.

'Maxime, I'm sorry you're upset, but truly, there's no need. Today, the three of us had a perfectly innocent picnic, that was all. Jan wanted . . . '

'Ah yes, Jan. You've stolen my son from me, too — just like Helen did.'

I paused in my packing.

'What d'you mean?' My voice sounded strained.

She continued her wandering, brushing past me, flicking shut my suitcase.

'Just like you, she stole my son's affections. Always laughing, joking.' Her voice became vindictive. 'Stupid girl, making eyes at Hugo, as if he would care.' She stopped, gazing into space dreamily. 'He might have done, mind you, if she had stayed.'

I could feel my throat tightening. Automatically, I resumed my packing.

'But Helen was an unhappy girl, I believe,' I murmured carefully. 'Broken-hearted over some man.'

'Was she?' For a moment she sounded almost interested.

'That's what you told the police.'

Suddenly, she turned on me. 'She was taking them away from me. Nobody cares about me, not my husband . . . not my child.' Her face looked spiteful. 'And Anna doesn't like me either.'

A terrible suspicion had taken hold of me, almost robbing me of speech, but I forced myself to answer her.

'That isn't true,' I said soothingly. 'Anna has never said a bad word about you. Hugo loves you, and so does Jan.'

'Nonsense!' Maxime shook her head wildly. 'Jan avoids me whenever he can. He liked Helen. He likes you, too. And he adored that revolting cat.'

I tried to edge away from her, towards the door. 'Yes, poor Mimi,' I said lightly. 'I wonder what happened to Mimi?'

She reached the door before me, and leaned against it, smiling. 'Well, I had to, didn't I? I couldn't let Jan care more for a cat than for his mother.'

I knew I must not look at her. If I did, she would read the horror I was feeling, and who knows what she might do. I snapped shut my case.

'There,' I said brightly. 'That's one case packed. I'll just put it outside the door, Maxime, and then I'll pack the other one.'

It was a good try, but it didn't work. She just stared at me, and made no effort to move out of my way.

'You don't think I'm going to let you go, do you?' She sneered. 'Not now, because you know, don't you? So you see, I can't let you go.'

'I don't know what you mean.' I faltered. 'Please Maxime, I haven't done you any harm. Can't we part as friends?'

She laughed. It was a harsh, gurgling laugh and it curdled my blood.

'But we are not parting, my poor little innocent,' she crooned. 'No, you will not be leaving Bruges. Not today. Not ever.'

'Please, Maxime. Move away from the door. I'm going out.'

For a moment, it seemed as though my bluff might work. She did move to one side, but as I put my hand on the door handle, she struck downwards with the edge of her hand on to my

126

wrist. The pain made me gasp, and as I clutched my wrist, she pushed me.

'You will pay, every one of you.' She was jabbing at me, hissing. 'I could have been famous, you know.' With her still poking at me, we circled around the bed. 'I could have been a great opera star,' she continued. 'I was already a star.'

'I know.' I gasped. 'Hugo told me you were wonderful. He said so. You were beautiful, and . . . '

'But he spoiled that.' She paid me no attention, lost in her own thoughts. 'Giving me a child! What did I want with a child? I could have had fame, applause, appreciation.'

Suddenly, she flung her arms wide, her face rapt, as though facing an imaginary audience. Then, just as suddenly, her arms dropped, and her expression became ugly. 'I didn't want to be dragged into domesticity. Hugo stole my life from me.'

'But, surely, once you had Jan . . . '

'It made me very ill,' she interrupted.

She looked at me with eyes as wide and innocent as a child. 'That was Jan's fault. I nearly died, all for a child who doesn't even like me.'

'You can't blame Jan. He's only a child. He's so little.'

'But Helen wasn't little. She was pretty though,' Maxime continued. 'And they all liked her. I can't think why. So you see, she had to go.'

We had reached the window. I was pressed up against it, and could go no farther but she just kept coming.

'Yes, she had to go. Just as you are going.'

It was now or never. I gave her a desperate push and tried to scramble over the bed away from her, but she flung herself on me. We struggled, and for all her air of fragility, she proved to be the stronger. I think I called for Hugo, even though I knew he was not in the house.

She was going to kill me! Even as I fought with her, and felt her hands clawing at my throat, the thought spun through my head that this could not be happening. I would wake up in a moment to find the whole thing was a bad dream.

But it had happened in reality to Helen. She had died, and so had Mimi, and Maxime had tried to kill me once before at the bell tower! I realised that now. I had to get away from her, to warn the others. She was quite mad, and there was no knowing what she might do to Anna or Jan, while she was like this.

With a final great heave, I managed to push Maxime away from me. We both went crashing to the floor, but I scrambled to my feet hurriedly. She was after me like a flash. I saw her reach out, and as if in slow motion, saw her pick up a bronze ornament. It was so heavy it was all she could do to raise it over her head. I swung around to avoid it, but it came crashing down.

There was blinding pain and everything went black. I knew I was falling, knew she had hit me, but there was nothing I could do to save myself. The last thing I heard before I lost consciousness was the grating sound of a window being pushed open.

8

'Sara! Come on . . . you're all right. Please wake up.'

Hands were tugging at me as I opened my eyes. Below me, I could see the dark waters of the canal. It didn't register at first, and then everything flooded back. I was hanging half out of the bedroom window, my head and arms actually over the edge.

'Let go of me! Don't you dare.' With a terrified cry, I twisted around and lashed out at the hands that held me.

'Sara, it's me, Anna. You're all right, my dear. Come, let me help you.'

'Anna! Oh, thank goodness. Where's Maxime? She . . . she tried to kill me.'

I let Anna help me back into the room, where I collapsed on to the bed. She smoothed back my hair.

'You've got a nasty bruise there. Big bump, coming up like an egg.'

'She hit me with something, the ornament . . . but what happened? Where is she now?'

'Hush now, and stay still a minute.'

Anna pushed me back on to the bed, and quickly held my flannel under the cold tap. She wrung it out and placed it on my forehead.

'I came up, just in time. I heard all the shouting, banging, bumping. Lucky I came.'

'Oh Anna!' I suddenly found myself near to tears.

She looked down at me anxiously. 'She was pushing you out of the window. I couldn't believe it. When I asked her what she was doing, she stopped, and ran out.'

I removed the flannel, and felt the bump on my head.

'Helen had a bruise on her head, too, didn't she?' I looked at Anna. 'Maxime killed Helen you know . . . she told me. She's sick, Anna. Quite mad.'

Anna went white. 'Oh, no! Jan! I left him in the kitchen on his own.'

She turned with surprising speed and flew down the stairs, with me hard on her heels. The kitchen door was open. So was the front door, and there was no sign of Jan!

'She's taken him.' I exclaimed.

We stared at one another. 'Perhaps she's gone up to her room.' Anna suggested. 'I'll go look.'

'No. I'm sure she's gone out.' I was thinking hard. What would Maxime be thinking? What had she intended, taking Jan?

'She wouldn't hurt her own son, would she?' Anna was shaking now.

I avoided her eyes. 'No, of course not.'

But I wasn't so sure. Maxime held that dear little boy responsible for her lost career. And she had vowed vengeance on us all, including him. There was no time to lose. I held Anna by the shoulders, looking into her eyes, making her realise the importance of what I was going to say.

'You must phone the police, Anna.'

'The police? Oh, no! Monsieur Hugo would not want . . . '

'You must. And you must try to contact Hugo. Do it, Anna, and quickly.'

'But what are you doing? Where are you going?'

I was already on my way down the hallway. 'I'm going after them. They can't be far. Someone may have seen them. I must find them. Phone now. Hurry!' I turned and ran towards the front door, unaware of the figure there until I crashed into it.

'Sara, whoa! What are you doing?'

Hugo! He was here, thank goodness! I clung to him, trying to explain. His arms closed about me and all I wanted was to stay there, safe and secure. But I had to make him understand.

'What's the matter?' he was asking, anxious now. 'Sara, what's happened to your head?'

'It's Maxime. She's got Jan. We've got to find her. Anna's phoning the police now.'

'The police? What d'you mean?'

'There isn't time to explain now. We must find them. Jan is in danger. Come on.'

He didn't argue further, but followed me. We looked up and down the deserted street, but Maxime was nowhere in sight.

'We'll have to split up,' Hugo said. 'What was Maxime wearing?'

'Black, and Jan is in red. The same as he had on earlier. Is there any place she might have gone?'

He shook his head. 'Sara. Tell me one thing.' His eyes, dark with pain, held mine. 'Was it Maxime who killed Helen? Has it been her all along?'

I nodded. 'I'm sorry, Hugo.'

He closed his eyes for a moment. 'Does Anna know what to tell the police?' When he spoke at last, his voice was completely calm.

'Yes, she knows it all. Hugo, you go that way. I'll take the streets to the left. She can't have gone far, not with Jan. He must be tired enough already.'

Suddenly he clasped me to him. 'Take care,' he muttered, then ran off one way. I went in the other direction.

I ran frantically through the streets, stopping people, trying to get help. Had any of them seen a woman in a black dress, a woman with smooth silvery hair and a little boy dressed in red?

Some of them didn't understand me, shrugged their shoulders and walked on. Others tried to help, but they weren't sure . . . they might have . . . I concentrated on all the streets that led up to the main thoroughfare, glancing up side roads, hoping all the time to see them, but no luck. Maxime could have dodged into a shop, of course, or gone into a church, even a café! They could be sitting quite calmly drinking lemonade or a milk shake.

Could she be climbing the steps of the tower? The sudden thought stopped me in my tracks, then sent me hurtling on, gasping for breath, my heart pounding. The tower had been her choice for me. I realised now that she had deliberately planted the idea of my going there into my mind, even giving me her camera to make sure I climbed to the top for the best views. It was Maxime who had pushed me! She'd been the dark figure that had rushed past me that day!

She had used a migraine as an excuse for Anna to look after Jan so that she could follow me to the tower. It was a plan conceived in the mind of a sick, tormented woman, and now she had little Jan at her mercy . . .

Was it possible that she might take Jan to the tower? Was her plan to put him in danger the same way as she had with me! I had to go there, and quickly.

I was out of breath by the time I reached the Halles, but I panted out my questions to the doorman.

'Has a woman climbed the tower? A woman with a small boy about four years old?'

The man behind the grille shook his head. 'There have been few up there today. A couple of American tourists

are there now, and some schoolchil-
dren.'

I had been so sure I was right that I
just gaped at him, disbelieving. 'Are you
positive?'

He raised his eyebrows. 'Quite. I
would have remembered. It is a long
climb for little legs. I would have said
something.'

I persisted. 'But if your back had
been turned, perhaps. Could anyone
have gone up without you knowing?
Can I go up and see?'

'If you pay, mademoiselle. Anyone
can go up if they pay.'

I hadn't any purse with me! 'It's very
important,' I cried. 'A matter of life and
death.'

Perhaps he read the fear in my face.
He shrugged and nodded. 'Go on then.
Look for yourself. But I tell you, they're
not up there.'

I pounded up the steps, meeting the
American tourists now on their way
down. By the time I reached the top, I
was nearly on my knees. But I had

looked everywhere. And the only people on the roof were the school kids.

I leaned against the parapet gasping for breath. I had been wrong . . . but where could she be? Then, while I was staring down at the square, I spotted them, like tiny toy figures. Maxime was unmistakable, and little Jan. She had him by the hand, almost dragging him as he pulled at her arm.

I could have wept with frustration. If I hadn't insisted on climbing the tower, I would have been able to catch up with them. Now there was nothing I could do. No-one below would hear me if I shouted, 'Stop that woman!'

I began clattering down the stairs again. When at last I reached the bottom, the door-keeper was waiting for me. 'You see. They weren't there, didn't I tell you.'

'But I've seen them.' I thanked him, and made him promise that if Maxime and Jan did return, he would not let them go up the tower. 'Call the police . . . anything . . . but don't let them go up there. The child is in danger.'

Out in the square, I was about to follow in Maxime's direction when I noticed there appeared to be more police about than usual. Two of them were walking across, in front of the Halles, and another one questioning a flower-seller.

'Are you looking for a Madame Rogier?' I asked one of them.

The officer gave me a sharp glance. 'We are. Are you the English girl, Sara Hastings?'

'Yes, but never mind that now. You've just missed her. I saw her from the top of the tower. She was with Jan, and they were going that way.'

I pointed to where I'd seen Maxime heading. The policeman called to the others, and gave quick instructions. Then he turned back to me.

'You say this woman attacked you?'

I pointed to the bump on my head.

'And what about some other girl who was found in the canal?'

'I'll tell you all about that later,' I

cried. 'Don't you understand? Madam Rogier is sick. She is not responsible for what she might do. And she has the child.'

He seemed to get the message, and we set off together down the street. Coming the other way, to my relief, we saw one of the other policemen with Hugo. When he saw me, he held out his hands, and as I clasped them in mine, I wasn't caring what anyone might think.

'I'm told you've spotted them,' he said. 'Was Jan all right?'

I nodded. 'They went this way. We'll catch them if we hurry.'

'No. I've just come along this street. I'd have seen them.' He turned to the police officer. 'My wife must have cut down one of the side streets.'

'My men are looking,' the officer said. 'Why don't you and Miss Hastings go home? There is nothing you can do here.'

He left us, standing helplessly, just staring at one another.

'Perhaps we had better go back,' he

said. 'You never know. Maxime might have returned.'

'Perhaps.'

I shivered 'It's a good thing Jan is still wearing his anorak,' I said lamely. 'It's gone quite cold.'

Hugo didn't answer, only squeezed my hand, and I knew that he could not trust himself to speak. We began back slowly.

I couldn't help wondering if any of the passers-by had seen them. Then I noticed a street artist, stationed at the corner there. He was a man who, by his very occupation, was trained to notice things. I dragged at Hugo's hand.

'Over here,' I said excitedly. 'Let's ask him.'

Had he seen a woman in black, and a small child, we asked him. The child was in red. The woman had striking looks.

'Beautiful, but distraite, n'est ce pas?'

'You've seen them?' I thought Hugo was going to pick the man up and kiss him!

The artist nodded. 'I was curious. She was unusual . . . something in her expression. I thought it was strange. The little boy was crying quietly, but she did not appear to notice.'

'Which way did they go?' Hugo demanded.

The man used his paintbrush to point to the street on his right. 'Down there, monsieur. Towards the canal.'

'Come on, Sara, hurry.'

Where were the police now? Just when we wanted them, they appeared to have vanished into thin air. We ran along the pavement, dodging shoppers, running in the road more often than not, until we reached the bridge.

We skidded to a halt there, looking both ways, but there was no sign of them.

'They can't be far away.'

I was straining my eyes, willing myself to find them. Along both banks of the canal people were walking, but not Maxime and Jan.

'Perhaps they've gone on one of the

boat tours?' I suggested.

He shook his head. 'They don't pick up here. These are all private boats.'

There weren't many of those either, just a couple, tied up to a small landing-stage. But there was a rowing-boat, pulling out to the middle . . .

'Hugo! It's them. Look! In the rowing-boat.'

It was Maxime all right, and the red of Jan's clothes stood out brightly. The boat was moving in a zig-zag direction as Maxime struggled with the oars. From the way they splashed, it was obvious she wasn't used to rowing, but she was pulling away steadily.

'She's got to come in to land eventually,' Hugo said. 'We'll follow.'

'But which side? And what about where the houses come right down to the water's edge?'

'Then we'll have to make a detour, and catch up again where we can. She won't be able to land there either.'

'We'd better each take one side of the

canal,' I said. 'We must keep up with them.'

'Right!' He started away, but then turned to me. 'Just keep them in view. If you see the police, call them. And Sara, if Maxime lands, don't go near her.'

I nodded and set off. I hardly needed telling. Nothing was going to persuade me to go near Maxime again.

I walked along the left bank, trying not to hurry, looking like someone out for a stroll. I hoped Maxime would not recognise me. She was holding a course more or less along the middle of the canal, but then she seemed to be veering over to the opposite side. I heaved a sigh of relief.

Hugo was there, and it wasn't long before she spotted him. I saw her head come up, her body stiffen. He was in full view, just as I was. She half rose in the boat, and screamed something I couldn't hear.

Hugo ran to the edge of the water, shouting to her. Her immediate response was to pull desperately on one oar, and swing the boat around. Now she was heading in my direction. I looked quickly up and down the path. No sign of any police, and it would take too long for Hugo to run around and cross by the bridge to this side. Even if he did, Maxime would only cross the water again. How long could she keep this up?

Just then, a man appeared round a bend in the path. I stepped right in front of him.

'Monsieur, would you help me, please?' I asked desperately.

He stopped.

'You see the woman in that boat?' I said, pointing. 'The police are looking for her. She must be brought ashore before she harms the child.'

He hesitated. 'What d'you want me to do about it,' he stammered. 'It is nothing to do with me.'

'Please, please. Just find a policeman. It is most important.'

'I will see what I can do,' he said and walked on. Maxime was still coming towards me, only yards from the bank.

She hadn't yet seen me because her back was towards me, but Jan must have recognised me. He scrambled to his feet, and the boat rocked wildly.

'Sara, Sara!' he yelled.

Maxime looked around then and stopped rowing. The boat went on gliding towards me, nearer and nearer. I saw her look wildly to the other bank and back again to me. She was trapped.

I went right up to the edge of the water. 'Maxime,' I shouted, 'bring Jan back. It's all right. Please, please bring him back.'

I could see Hugo running along the other bank. It would take him some time to cross by the bridge and reach us. All I could do was keep her here . . . Keep her talking.

'Maxime, please come ashore. You need help. Let us help you.'

Leaving go of the oars, she stood up in the boat, barely keeping her balance. She grabbed hold of Jan by his shoulders.

'Go away!' she screamed. 'Go away!

You and Hugo. Go right away from me or I'll throw Jan in.'

'No!' I backed away. Perhaps she was only bluffing, but Jan was sobbing with fright and I couldn't risk it. 'I'm going. Look, Maxime, I'm going.'

She still held Jan, but he tried to pull away from her. The boat began to sway.

'Maxime, sit down!' I yelled.

It was too late. Whether she really tried to push Jan into the water or not I couldn't be sure, but the boat tilted. Jan screamed and clutched at her. The next moment, the boat capsized.

They both went under immediately. I had no idea if Maxime could swim and I was sure Jan could not. I kicked off my shoes and dived in.

I was quite a strong swimmer but I wasn't used to swimming fully clothed. The water weighed me down and sucked at my legs. I struck out for the spot where they had vanished, desperately kicking, diving under the surface to try to find Jan.

At last, to my relief, I spotted his red

anorak. I reached him, grabbing hold of the hood. He was threshing about, but I was able to keep him at arm's length, and there was enough air trapped in his waterproof jacket to give him some buoyancy.

'Lie still,' I gasped. 'Lie still, Jan. You're safe now.'

I started to kick my way to the bank when I saw Maxime. She had come up not far from us, and was trying to reach us. Her long arms were clawing at the water.

I don't think she even realised her danger. Her eyes were blazing with hatred and she was intent on making her way towards us. I knew then that if she reached us, we would all die together.

'Keep away,' I screamed.

Desperation lent strength to my limbs and I kicked out harder than ever. Then I heard voices and realised with relief that I had reached the bank. Hands reached out to lift Jan from the water and drag me, coughing and spluttering, on to dry land. A man was already carrying Jan in his arms.

'Is Jan all right? Where are you taking him?' I panted.

Someone threw a blanket round my shoulders. 'He'll be fine. An ambulance is on its way,' a voice said.

I saw Hugo running towards us, and I turned to look for Maxime. She was still floundering in the water. I am sure she saw Hugo as she flung up her arms and vanished beneath the water. Hugo was stripping off his jacket.

'No,' I screamed. 'No, Hugo. She'll pull you down.'

He paid no attention, as he took a running dive into the canal. He, too, disappeared beneath the murky water . . .

9

I turned desperately for help. The police had at last caught up with us, and were putting Jan into an ambulance.

'You must come, too, mademoiselle,' one of them said.

'But Hugo . . . '

'Monsieur is all right. See, there he is.'

I saw Hugo surface, look wildly around him, before diving again. Then I saw no more because they hurried me away, saying that Jan would need me.

I sat beside the child, holding his tiny hand while the ambulance pulled away from the canal and proceeded at breakneck speed through the narrow Bruges streets.

'Sara?' His voice quavered, then he burst into tears, flinging his arms around my neck.

When we reached the hospital, Jan

was taken away from me. Promising that I would see him in the morning, and having been reassured that he was none the worse physically for his ordeal, I allowed a nurse to lead me away. There was the luxury of a hot bath, then examinations and an injection.

'Canal water is not the healthiest thing to drink quantities of,' I was told.

My sodden clothes had been taken from me and I was modestly clad in a hospital robe.

'I want to go home,' I objected. 'There's nothing wrong with me.'

'Tomorrow,' the nurse said soothingly. 'Tonight Jan Rogier must stay in for observation. And so must you.'

I was tucked into bed in a general ward and curtains were pulled around me.

'Try to get some sleep,' she said, then left.

How could I sleep! What had happened to Hugo? I didn't even know whether they had fished Maxime out of the canal. Pictures kept flickering through my mind. Maxime, her hand upraised, the bronze ornament about to come down on my head. Maxime, standing in the boat, threatening to push Jan overboard.

I had been such a fool. All the time I had never suspected her, had half believed the things she had said about Hugo, taken in by her friendly attitude, her insistence that I make myself attractive. I should have realised . . . known she was unbalanced . . . known her story about Helen's broken heart could not be true.

She had been such a good actress. What would she say to the police, I wondered. She would deny everything. Maybe even accuse me of making things up out of jealousy over Hugo. Then I remembered that Anna had seen her attempting to push me out of the window. There could be no denying that.

Whether it was sheer exhaustion, or something in the injection, I don't know, but I did fall asleep. It must have

been hours later when I woke to find
Anna sitting beside my bed, dressed in
her best black and cherry-trimmed hat.
I reached out and touched her hand.

'Anna!'

'So, you're with us again,' she said.
'You bear a charmed life. How are you?'

'Nothing wrong with me,' I replied. I
found the courage to ask the question I
dreaded. 'And Hugo?'

She patted my hand. 'He is well. He
has seen his son. The poor little thing is
fast asleep. Tomorrow Jan can come
home. You can both come home.'

There was something else I had to
ask. 'And Maxime?'

She evaded my eyes. 'The police
found her, eventually.'

'What d'you mean?' I tried to sit up.

'Hush, do not excite yourself.'

She pushed me back against the
pillows, fussing, making me comfortable, but I gripped her arm.

'It was too late,' she said reluctantly.
'Monsieur Hugo dived and dived like
someone crazy. There were others

searching the canal, too.' She gave a heavy sigh. 'When they brought her up, it was too late.'

'Oh, Anna. Poor Maxime. Poor Hugo.'

'It was better,' she said fiercely. 'Bad enough for him now, answering all these questions the police ask. Better for him. Better for her.'

Anna sighed. 'It is hard to believe. But, enough for now. Tonight you must rest. Tomorrow the police wish to speak with you.'

'With me?'

'But naturally. It is to you Maxime confessed, n'est ce pas? The police wished to interview you tonight, but Hugo persuaded them. He is with them instead.'

She stood up, shaking her head sadly. 'It has been a terrible thing, but you must put it behind you. Tomorrow Mr Hugo will want to talk to you also.'

'Very well,' I agreed weakly. 'Thank you for coming, Anna.'

A faint smile found its way into her

eyes. 'It will be nice to have you back, my dear.'

She found her way through the curtains that still enclosed my bed, and left me lying there filled with misgivings. Somehow the thought that Maxime might have drowned had never entered my head. To me, she had become such a threatening figure, that she had seemed invincible. When Hugo had dived after her, my only dread had been that she would pull him under. And now she was dead . . .

What would Hugo say to me when we met? Would he blame me for Maxime's death? Perhaps if I had never come here; had not pretended to be plain; had not allowed Maxime to penetrate my disguise and so whet her appetite for jealousy, all this would never have happened.

Then I told myself not to be foolish. The seeds of Maxime's tragedy had been sown a long time ago. Who knows when it had all begun, perhaps even when Hugo had fallen under Maxime's spell and persuaded her to marry him.

I wondered if Hugo was thinking the same. If he was blaming himself, he was wrong. There had been something unbalanced in Maxime right from the beginning, otherwise she would not have reacted the way she did to marriage and motherhood. Maxime had retreated into a world of crazy bitterness as a result of her situation and frustrations.

Better that Hugo should blame me than go through the rest of his life blaming himself. He would have to live with this, whereas I could return to England and forget all about it.

Next morning, I woke up feeling stiff but otherwise perfectly fit. I persuaded the Ward Sister to let me visit Jan, and found him washed and tidied and ready for some breakfast. His face lit up when he saw me.

'We're going home soon,' I told him.

To my surprise, he looked away and I saw him tense.

'Don't want to go home.'

I guessed what was troubling him. 'Anna will be missing you. I bet she's making some gingerbread men.'

He still didn't say anything.

'And Daddy will be coming, in his car.'

There was a struggle going on inside. At last he broke his silence. 'And Mama?' There was a tremor in his voice.

'Mama won't be there, Jan.' I stroked his hair. 'She's gone away.'

'Like Mimi?'

I winced. 'Something like that. Daddy will explain.'

'But you'll be there?'

I hesitated. What could I answer? My own future was so uncertain, but I guessed that Hugo would not want me around to remind him of these terrible events.

'I'll be here, at least for a while,' I promised, and he seemed satisfied.

When Hugo came, he brought with him a bag of fresh clothes for both of us. I went back to my own ward to dress. I then collected Jan, once he was ready, and we went together into the reception area. Jan flung himself at his father, who held his son very close. Over Jan's shoulder, his eyes met mine, and I could see his face was tired and serious.

'Are you all right?' he asked gently.

'Fine,' I assured him. 'And you?'

He gave a faint smile. 'As well as can be expected, I think is the expression.'

We walked outside to the car, and I couldn't think what to say. I ought to tell him I knew about Maxime, but I could not bring myself to.

The house near the Quai Vert was still the same. I don't know why I thought it should be otherwise. It just seemed that something should register the events that had taken place.

Anna, who had been polishing and baking with ferocious energy, took us into the kitchen, where she'd made tea. Jan was quiet and apprehensive at first, but soon began to relax.

'I've something for you, son,' Hugo said.

From a box, he lifted a little black ball of fluff. It wriggled and stretched, opened a little pink mouth and mewed.

'For me?' Jan jumped up in excitement. He took the kitten and held it against his face. 'What will you call him?' I asked.

Jan thought hard, then smiled triumphantly. 'I'll call him Rosebud.'

'Rosebud!' His father exploded with laughter. It was as though it was a relief for him to find something to laugh about. 'Why Rosebud?'

'Because I like it,' Jan said firmly.

★ ★ ★

The police were very kind towards me. We went over and over the happenings of the past few weeks, and at last they gave me a statement to sign.

'What will happen?' I asked the officer.

He shrugged. 'It is not up to me. But I would say nothing.'

I was glad. I would have given

anything to see Hugo smiling again, as carefree as he had been on the boat to Damme. For such a brief moment, we had all been happy. It seemed a lifetime away now.

I didn't see much of Hugo during the day. There were many arrangements to be made, people to be informed. He was out of the house most of the time, no doubt using the office as his base. Time passed quietly for the rest of us. Not knowing what else to do, I helped Anna turn out some of the rooms, cleaning and polishing.

We gave Jan a cotton reel on a length of string, and he played with Rosebud until bedtime. Only then did he show signs of distress. I stayed with him, reading to him until he fell asleep.

'I could make you up a bed in the room next door,' Anna suggested, 'in case he should wake in the night.'

I accepted the idea gratefully. I wasn't too keen on my own room any more. It held too many disturbing memories. I helped Anna, and afterwards she went off to her own quarters, and I settled down with a book. Anna had lit a fire, and it was burning brightly, sending out a comforting warmth.

I was still there when Hugo came home.

'A fire . . . good. It's getting chilly outside now.'

He dropped into a chair, stretched his long legs towards the blaze and closed his eyes. I went quietly to the drinks cabinet and poured him a brandy.

'Here, this will do you good.'

He took it, cradling the glass between his hands, staring into the fire.

'I should have known,' he said at last.

I remained silent. He was talking to himself as much as to me.

'It was my fault. I should have realised — '

'But how could you?' I interrupted. 'Nobody would have guessed.'

He shook his head. 'I should. Maxime . . . ' He faltered as he used his wife's name, and then continued.

'Maxime had a volatile character. There were often rages.'

'But many people are like that,' I pointed out, 'particularly those who are gifted. Maybe she became jealous through boredom.'

'But perhaps not so obsessively jealous.'

He rose to his feet and began to pace backwards and forwards.

'She was jealous of anybody or anything she thought might usurp her. From the time Jan was born, she was jealous of her own son. I dared not pay him too much attention.'

I poured myself a drink, too, and sat quietly sipping it. Hugo needed to talk like this, though, for myself, I would rather have tried to push the whole thing out of my mind. For him, that would be impossible.

He went on. 'I thought perhaps if Jan had a nanny, Maxime would not feel so trapped.'

We all knew what the outcome of that had been.

'I knew she was jealous of Helen,' he said, 'though she had no need to be. Helen was just a nice, ordinary girl.' He turned to me. 'I swear there was nothing . . . '

'I know,' I said quickly. 'I know.'

He tossed back his drink, and laid down the glass. 'There were the usual scenes.' He glanced at me. 'I expect you heard one the other night. It was after Jan let slip that we had all had coffee together. Maxime flew at me like a wild thing.' He looked down at his hand.

And I had thought his hand had been scratched by Mimi!

'But when Helen was found drowned,' I prompted, 'didn't you wonder?'

He gave a bitter laugh. 'You'd think I would have done, but no, I didn't. Perhaps I deliberately refused to allow myself to suspect anything,' he said slowly. 'I believed what Maxime said Helen had told her about a lover. I could not — would not — believe that Helen's death had anything to do with us.'

'So that was why you advertised for a plain girl? So that Maxime would not be jealous.'

Hugo sighed. 'It sounds naive, doesn't it?'

He came and sat beside me on the sofa. 'I was torn both ways. Jan, I could see, needed somebody stable. His mother either ignored him or became too possessive. I did hope that this time it might work.'

His voice tailed away. We both knew how vain such a hope had been.

'You see now,' he said quietly, 'why I ignored you so pointedly at first. And why I shouted at Jan when he gave so much affection to his cat.'

'Even poor Mimi . . . ' I murmured.

'Even Mimi,' he repeated. 'I really did begin to wonder then. I was afraid of what I had done, bringing you here. I had to watch over you.'

'And that was why you always seemed to be around?'

'Yes, after your mishap in the bell tower, but I still could not bring myself to believe it of my own wife.'

So that was why he came on the trip to Damme! It had not been from a need for my company. Why should I think it was?

He took hold of my hand, cradling it in his own. 'You saved Jan's life. I can never thank you enough. And you nearly lost your own. Can you ever forgive me for my blindness? I was a stupid, careless man.'

Now it was my turn to pull away and jump up. I crossed to the fireplace, leaning against the mantelpiece, staring down into the fire. I didn't want his gratitude, or his apologies.

'There is nothing to forgive,' I said flatly. 'Anyone would have done the same.'

I sought wildly for something to say, something to change the topic of conversation. But I couldn't think of anything. It was Hugo who said something that surprised me.

'I'm going to sell this house.'

I turned to face him. 'But I thought you loved it.'

'Why should you think that? It was Maxime's choice. I always found it too gloomy.'

'But where will you go?'

'I've had my eye on a smaller place, near the park of the Minnewater.' For the first time that evening, his expression became animated, the lines of strain softening. 'There is a house there which looks on to green grass and trees.'

So, I thought bleakly, this would be it then. In a smaller house there would be no need for me. Anna would have less work to do and could look after Jan.

'You won't . . . you won't miss the canal, will you?' he asked.

I stared at him. 'Miss the canal?' Did he mean when I returned to England?

'You won't mind the house not being on the canal? I know you love the Bruges waterways.'

'I've gone off them a little,' I murmured. 'Let's get this right. You want me to come to the new house?'

Now it was his turn to look

surprised. 'But of course. Jan will need you.'

My heart sank. I would stay, naturally. Fool that I was. I would bury the pain of longing for a man who would never give me a second thought. It would be enough to be near him, and Jan. I loved that child, just as much as I loved his father.

'You will come, Sara?'

There as an urgency in his voice. I could understand his not wanting all the inconvenience of finding another nanny for Jan. And after all the things that had been happening, he might not find it so easy.

I turned back to the fire. 'Oh, yes, I'll come,' I said finally.

I heard him rise and thought he was about to leave the room, now that the arrangements for his son had been made to his satisfaction, but then I felt him behind me, taking hold of me by the shoulders.

He turned me round to face him. 'Sara?'

I didn't want to look up. I could feel

a stupid tear trickling down my cheek.

I sniffed. 'I'm sorry. It's been a trying time . . . but worse for you.'

'Sara.' He repeated my name and, taking a handkerchief from his pocket, he gently wiped away the tear. 'Look at me.'

Reluctantly, I raised my eyes. He touched my face, running his fingertips along the line of my jaw.

'There are things I shall want to say, to you, my sweet Sara. Things I have wanted to say from the very beginning.'

He smiled gently, and a little glow of warmth started somewhere in the centre of me.

'But now is not the right time, is it? D'you know what I mean?'

I nodded. 'I think so . . . and you are quite right, Hugo. This is not the right time.'

'But the day will come, when the time and the place *will* be right.' He looked a little anxious. 'In the meantime, we need you, Jan and I. Will you wait?'

I took a deep breath. Hugo, I knew, must have time to grieve for a love that had turned to bitter regret. He had to work through feelings of guilt and pain. But one day, the shadow of the past would disappear, and he would be able to live and love again. When that time came, I would be there.

'I can wait,' I said quietly, 'for as long as it takes.'

There was only a sudden intake of breath on his part, a tightening of his fingers where he held my shoulders. But it was enough to tell me all I needed to know.

The door opened, and an anxious pyjama-clad figure clutching a sleepy kitten, stood looking wide-eyed at us.

'Rosebud was wondering where you were?' he said accusingly.

His father swept them both up into his arms, and then held out a hand to me.

'Back to bed, young man. And don't worry. We're both here.' His fingers closed around mine, and there was a wonderful new certainty in his voice. 'We'll always be here, won't we, Sara?'

I could hear the familiar carillon ringing faintly in the dark, over the rooftops of Bruges. This time, its happy tune did not seem at all out of place.

'Always,' I said firmly. 'For ever and ever. Jan, Daddy, Anna and Sara.'

'And Rosebud,' Jan said with great satisfaction.

THE END

We do hope that you have enjoyed reading this large print book.

Did you know that all of our titles are available for purchase?

We publish a wide range of high quality large print books including:
Romances, Mysteries, Classics
General Fiction
Non Fiction and Westerns

Special interest titles available in large print are:
The Little Oxford Dictionary
Music Book, Song Book
Hymn Book, Service Book

Also available from us courtesy of Oxford University Press:
Young Readers' Dictionary
(large print edition)
Young Readers' Thesaurus
(large print edition)

For further information or a free brochure, please contact us at:
Ulverscroft Large Print Books Ltd.,
The Green, Bradgate Road, Anstey,
Leicester, LE7 7FU, England.
Tel: (00 44) **0116 236 4325**
Fax: (00 44) **0116 234 0205**

VISIONS OF THE HEART

Christine Briscomb

When property developer Connor Grant contracted Natalie Jensen to landscape the grounds of his large country house near Ashley in South Australia, she was ecstatic. But then she discovered he was acquiring — and ripping apart — great swathes of the town. Her own mother's house and the hall where the drama group met were two of his targets. Natalie was desperate to stop Connor's plans — but she also had to fight the powerful attraction flowing between them.

FINGALA, MAID OF RATHAY

Mary Cummins

On his deathbed, Sir James Montgomery of Rathay asks his daughter, Fingala, to swear that she will not honour her marriage contract until her brother Patrick, the new heir, returns from serving the King. Patrick must marry. Rathay must not be left without a mistress. But Patrick has fallen in love with the Lady Catherine Gordon whom the King, James IV, has given in marriage to the young man who claims to be Richard of York, one of the princes in the Tower.

ZABILLET OF THE SNOW

Catherine Darby

For Zabillet, a young peasant girl growing up in the tiny French village of Fromage in the mid-fourteenth century, a respectable marriage is the height of her parents' ambitions for her. But life is changing. Zabillet's love for a handsome shepherd is tested when she is invited to join the La Neige household, where her mistress, Lady Petronella, has plans for her grandson, Benet. And over all broods the horror of the Great Death that claims all whom it touches.

PERILOUS JOURNEY

Caroline Joyce

After the execution of Charles I, Louisa's Royalist father considers it too dangerous for her to stay in England and arranges for her to go to the Isle of Man with Armand de la Tremouille, the nephew of the island's Royalist Governor. Their ship is boarded by Parliamentarians who plan to sail for Ireland, but a storm causes them to be shipwrecked on the Calf of Man. Magnus Stapleton, the Parliamentarian chief, becomes infatuated with Louisa, but she has fallen in love with Armand.

THE GYPSY'S RETURN

Sara Judge

After the death of her cruel father, Amy Keene's stepbrother and stepsister treated her just as badly. Amy had two friends, old Dr. Hilland and the washerwoman, Rosalind, with her fatherless child Becky. When Rosalind falls ill, Amy is entrusted with a letter to be given to Becky on her marriage. When the letter's contents are discovered, it causes Amy both mental and physical suffering and sets the seal of fate upon Rosalind's gypsy friend, Elias Jones.

WEB OF DECEIT

Margaret McDonagh

A good-looking man turned up on Louise's doorstep one day, introducing himself as Daniel Kinsella, an Australian friend of her brother-in-law, Greg. He said he had come to stay whilst he did some research — apparently Greg had written to her about it. Louise's initial reaction was to turn him away, but he was very persuasive. However, she was to discover that Daniel had bluffed his way into her life, and soon she found herself caught up in his dangerous mission.